THE HIDDEN RELIGION:

ERIC'S FALLEN GRACE

THE HIDDEN RELIGION:

ERIC'S FALLEN GRACE

D.R. HAMILTON

CHAPTER I

KING OF THE DESERT

Camp Dwyer, Marine base, Iran

Before the twilight of the first morning light, the subtle sound of running shoes pounding against the paved path is barely audible; as the runner heavily breathes in and out, he clears his mind of the drably painted military barracks that he quietly passes. He scans through the options on his smart watch; 4:25 am, the time blinks. The runner turns and heads back to his barrack.

In his barrack, a digital alarm clock noisily disturbs the stillness of an empty room. The cracked white painted door to that barrack is quickly pushed open, and a fit soldier enters with sweat beaded on his forehead. As the sweat gathers and dots, his light brown hair sticks to his skin. The camel-colored shirt he wore clings to his toned heaving chest.

He takes a moment to scan his room; he looks around the barrack to ensure everything is as he left it. His instinct to identify threats and notice when something appears out of place has always been an asset to him. He closes his eyes and begins to slow his heart rate and breath. In his mind, he reviews the picture of his room before he leaves. He then opens his eyes and gazes around the room; the bed is folded in place, the sheets are tightly tucked under the mattress, and the right corner is folded back at the top of the bed. Satisfied, he relaxed, and the dog tags clinked together as he slowly began removing his sweaty shirt, revealing his toned muscular chest. On the left side of his chest is a tattoo of an angry two head dog. Written underneath are the words USMC Hell Hounds. He now walks into the bathroom, gauges himself bluntly in the mirror, peers at his dog tags, Sergeant Eric Lansing; RECON is stamped on them.

Eric puts the lid down on the toilet seat and sits down to remove his running shoes; he then stands and drops his pants to the floor before stepping into the shower. He turns on the water, which comes out cold against the heat of his skin from the morning run. The cold water is a shock to your system, keeps your skin from wrinkling, and keeps you alert and ready, Eric thought to himself.

Eric grabs the bar of soap and runs it over his chest and abdomen. He begins to ponder; the desert sun was hotter here on the base than in most places in the world. Folks back home wouldn't be able to live with it. They probably would stay inside and watch TV to avoid it. Eric saw the sun and heat as a challenge, and it was up to him to adapt to the climate. However, the desert did have some benefits, as it had provided him with a healthy, light bronze skin tone. Eric placed his head directly under the shower head as he took the bar of soap and lathered it to build up a lather in his hands. He began to run the soap through his hair and face, cleaning his thin brown mustache. The sun had also slightly lightened his hair color, as he now had a few highlighted strands throughout his hair and mustache.

He wasn't sure what type of soldier the engineers had in mind when they designed these ridiculously undersized showers, but he assumed it went along with the compact living space of the barracks on base. Every morning he had to do his best to pivot inside the showers to wash his back while washing off the sand and sweat from his run. He didn't mind the barely livable barracks, but he seriously despised the shower. It was hardly accommodating for a 6 foot 2, 195-pound former high school quarterback to bathe in.

Remembering the limited water rations, Eric shuts off the water, steps out of the shower, and begins to pat himself dry. Towel around his waist, he walks out the bathroom of his small dwelling. The barracks at Camp Dwyer were as mundane and sparse as one could have imagined a military barrack to be. They were constructed in a hurry by military engineers when the U.S. began its occupation of Iran. The rooms were white-painted fabricated wood and had small analog dialed swamp coolers cut into the walls. It was unbearably hot most of the time, and he began to wonder if they even worked; these swamp coolers didn't cool the room much. Although Eric's room was considered better than those of other soldiers, it wasn't better by much.

Besides his military equipment, Eric had only one personal item in his room, a single picture of his family; his mother, father, and sister. Opening a small drawer, he finds his clean, camouflage uniform trousers and puts them on. His clock alarm loudly beeps for a second time. Shirtless, he grins to himself, having beat the notice once again. Then, quickly silencing the alarm, he starts to put on the rest of his uniform.

Out of the corner of his eye, Eric notices a figure move past the curtain-drawn window next to his door. There is a hard knock at the door.

"Yes, Private?" Eric says as he opens the door to greet the visitor.

"Sir, are you Sergeant Lansing?" The private asks as he salutes.

"Yeah, that's me.," Eric responds curiously.

"Colonel Johnson wants me to drive you to the briefing tent at 0900 hours." the Private states."

"Thank you. Pick me up in front of the mess hall twenty before then?"

"Yes, sir." replies the Private.

The soldier hands Eric a slip of paper, salutes, and then walks off. Eric closes the door, opens the note, reads it, then tosses the letter on top of his drawer, and finishes dressing. After he is fully clothed, Eric decides he has just enough time to grab some coffee.

Eric had been stationed in different parts of the world, but he wasn't particularly fond of this base. He enjoyed the simplicity of his military surroundings. It allowed him to stay focused on what was important. And what was that? His team and their missions. Eric's team members were now his family. His Colonel might say that Eric had a flawless record. Without a doubt, he was successful at completing his missions, and everyone got home safe to their families. However, his Colonel might add, in private, that he often took some unnecessary risks. It was that reason he and his team were deployed here once again.

As Eric left his room, the desert sun began its rage above the scorching dry horizon. In the desert, a man may think he's the dominant force on earth, but the sun truly reigns uncontested here in the desert, Eric thought to himself. He continued his solo thoughts; that deadly sun was why I love to come here. I need to defeat my adversaries, but I also need to survive against the king of the desert.

CHAPTER II

SOMETHING OUT OF PLACE

It was a short distance from Eric's barracks to the mess hall. As he neared the doors to the mess hall, Eric glanced at soldiers nearby performing their morning drills or daily duties in the distance. Two MPs passed Eric in a jeep, and in a blatant attempt to intimidate him, they glared at him as they passed. Eric thought to himself, Military Police are the biggest assholes on every base, always trying to prove they're better than everyone else. As he walked into the building, he named those two MPs, Frick and Frack.

Although the mess hall was a sizable building, it was only large enough to allow the men to eat in shifts. Inside the mess hall, Eric briefly looked around and surveyed the room. To his liking, he realized it was still just a typical mess hall. The food trays were stacked directly to the left as you entered the front door. Behind the trays were pre-wrapped breakfast sandwiches. Eric decided when he first arrived never to eat those sandwiches for breakfast. He assumed the sandwiches were made from leftover meat from yesterday's breakfast chow. Behind the breakfast sandwich heating pan were the cooks shuffling about it. These guys were no longer enlisted men, but contractors paid to work here. They were wearing their usual white shirt, black pants, and white cotton apron.

To Eric's left was the juice dispenser, pre-packaged pastries brought in from the factories in the States. Across from there was the large coffee machine. Next to the coffee maker was nearly every flavor you could think of, Moose Double Dark Chocolate, Swiss Vanilla Almond, Mountain Fresh Kahlua, Sumatra Dark Roast, and French Roast. Eric walks over to the coffee machine, deposits one of the flavored cups in the dispenser, grabs a cup, and places it on the cup landing. He selects his quantity and waits as the coffee begins to pour. Eric's coffee pick was the Sumatra Dark roast. Some prefer those new flavors, but those flavors were more like dessert than coffee to Eric. Eric chose the dark-roasted coffees; he thought they had a bold, heavy flavor. Yes, sir, simple is the best, Eric thought to himself as he savored the aroma of the coffee pouring into his cup. Eric thought that the coffee was the only decent thing that this base had to offer. Deep down, he realized he mostly enjoyed coffee because it reminded him of the morning he would get up early to go fishing with his dad. His dad would use the old coffee maker in the morning to brew coffee, and Eric enjoyed the smell of the coffee brewing when he awoke.

Others may find the simple pleasure of enjoying a hot cup of brew in the mess hall boring, but it was a welcome change from the tension of being in the field. As he sipped on the hot coffee, Eric leaned on the table behind him, allowing himself to relax in the calm familiarity of the environment. Far off to his right, Eric checked the long tables where soldiers ate, except for a few guys cleaning up. The place was pretty empty. Yep, nothing out of place here. Eric happily thought to himself.

Eric hears the light tap of a jeep horn outside the mess hall. Not wanting to be late, he decides to finish the remaining coffee on the ride to the briefing. Eric was glad he chose not to walk with the sun heating things. On the way, he heard squad leaders yelling commands at the squads, ordering them to stay in formation as they jogged past him. Eric wonders if the guys know how good they have it - only taking orders and not having to be responsible for someone not making it home.

The private pulls up in front of the building where their briefing will be held. After thanking the driver, Eric hops out and enters the building in search of the Colonel's briefing room. Eric walks the halls attempting to locate the space. He begins to fondly remember the tough Colonel who spent so much time molding him into a leader. The Colonel made him sign up for one of those "Traits for Strong Leadership" training courses many years back. He didn't want to do it at first, but now he had to admit that learning to read the room has served him well, many times over. "Know your audience," the Colonel would sternly tell him, and "Presentations are just another type of battle. You'll learn that the same information had to be delivered differently to the squads, then to the top leaders." he would say. "Reading the faces of your audience is a skill few masters, even at my level," Eric remembers him saying. The Colonel was a true leader, tough as a lion, but also a patient mentor. He had shielded Eric on several occasions when others wanted his head.

As Eric approached the briefing room, he began to visualize the space. The room was about twenty feet by fifteen feet with white-colored walls. There was a long conference room-style table, with approximately ten chairs in the center of the room. There were seven chairs on the north side of the table and three chairs on the south side. The first chair sat alone on the west end of the table, which had an extension for tech equipment such as a laptop. There was a projector at the opposite end of the table. Across from the long table, towards the front of the room, was a smaller table with seating for four. He expected his commander to be at the front of the room, with a few other high brasses sitting around the table looking stern about some situation that went south and now needed to be cleaned up.

Stepping inside the doorway of the briefing room, he paused to survey the room as was his custom, and his expression instantly changed from the relaxed coffee drinker to that of a concerned expression. He immediately noticed things were out of place from expectations. Well, it wasn't precisely that some things were out of order. It was more like the attendees were out of place or unusual. Instead of his fire squad and a few commanding officers in attendance, two civilians were present. A young female redhead was sitting in the single chair on the west side of the table, working on a laptop, and a mature middle-aged man with his back turned to the entrance. He appeared to be on a mobile phone.

Eric decided he'd better assess the situation and civilians quickly. The young redhead was intently staring at her laptop screen and typing. Eric wagered that she was about the age of a college student, petite framed. She wore a black baseball cap, with her natural red shoulder-length hair twisted into one braid draped over her left shoulder. She wore silver rings, and her fingernails were painted flat black. She wore a white button-down blouse and an oversized dark gray blazer. The blouse and jacket sleeves were folded up to her forearm. On the back of her laptop was a sticker that Eric recognized. It was a red and white flat design of a winged serpent swallowing a military soldier. It was a sticker from a video game Eric played when he was younger, called "Covert Wars II: Queen of Demons." Didn't know that game was still around, Eric thought to himself.

The other unknown attendee was a tall, dark-haired male. Although his back was turned, Eric felt they were about the same height. The male visitor was dressed in an expensive dark blue fitted suit. When he turned around briefly, Eric could see the slacks and dark blue blazer were paired with a light blue pressed button-down shirt. Obviously, this guy was rich, and his suit was custom-tailored. Unfortunately, he was sorely out of place on this base and in this part of the world in general. If an enemy sniper were looking for a quick kill, he'd be an easy target.

He was also speaking quite softly on his mobile phone. Due to a potential security risk, cell phones weren't usually allowed to be turned on inside briefings. So whoever this guy is, it must be pretty crucial for the Colonel to allow him to use his mobile inside his conference room, Eric thought to himself. Eric didn't mind the guy being on the cell phone any more than he felt about most of today's devices being a big distraction from the world. Moments of life were missed by focusing on these devices, making the person an easy target for anyone looking to take advantage of a distracted person.

Eric looks at his commander standing at the front of the room. The commander shakes his head slightly from side to side to ward off Eric's concerns. Then, recognizing his commander's signal, he walks to the opposite side of the room from the visitors, sits his coffee cup down on a small table, leans himself against the wall, crossing his arms patiently as he waits for his team to arrive. In a moment, members of Eric's squad begin entering the room, single file; Sam, Cesar, then Darryl. Each member enters the room and notices the civilians, one by one; they turn a questioning gaze toward Eric. Eric shrugs and nods toward the chairs, signaling them to sit down.

As they pull out their chairs to sit, Eric passes the time by recounting their skillset and history in his mind. Sam Reiner is 5'8 from West Virginia, light brown beard that matches his hair. He is usually quiet, reserved, and hyper-focused. He was our sniper extraordinaire, simply one of the best damn long-range shooters around. His ability to find his targets was uncanny. You'd never suspect he could hit a nickel from the length of a football field. He was also our demolition explosives expert. I guess all that focus is essential when you're the one carrying around explosives.

Cesar Ramos is from southern California, 5'6, dark black hair, probably the most diminutive guy on the team, but with the biggest heart. He's the team grenadier. Due to his catholic upbringing, Cesar always says a prayer before the beginning of every mission. He says his beliefs help him always see the positive side of every situation, which can be helpful in a stressful situation. He's also the team linguist speaking several languages, including English, Spanish, and Arabic. Occasionally, he dabbles in Latin.

Darryl, second in command, is 6'3" from Illinois. He handles the heavier artillery suppression in a firefight. He loves discussing his favorite conspiracies, like reptiles are actually running the government, and the famous queen is an alien clone. This guy had a conspiracy theory for everything. His conspiracies always made for a good laugh. I often felt that thinking about all the conspiracies all day is why he doesn't have any hair. People in my small backwater hometown would call him threatening because of his height and complexion. But on this squad, we call him our brother.

After everyone is seated, the dark-haired civilian ends his phone call. The Commander begins the meeting by introducing everyone.

"Fire squad - Hell Hounds, this is Dominik Klatten and Grace from the Global Unity Corporation. Dominik is the biopharmaceutical division exec, and Grace is his principal technologies security officer. They have an important mission for the US military and this squad specifically."

The commander nods toward Dominik, who then begins to address everyone.

"Our corporation is attempting to acquire a biohazard that terrorists stole from one of our secure facilities. We've learned from our sources that those terrorists' cells are planning to use the material to attack a populated city here in Iran. The potential for mass casualties is high. Therefore, this material must be recovered, and those terrorists met with swift justice. The material is housed in containers that send out a unique signature. Usually, we would notify the FBI, but this is a highly sensitive matter; This could be a potential global catastrophe, so our corporation needed to act swiftly with a plan fit for this delicate issue."

He walks over to Grace and rests his hand on her left shoulder. Grace, obviously annoyed, moves her shoulder forward, allowing Dominik's hand to slip off her shoulder. Dominik continues speaking as if nothing happened.

"Using our company satellites and advanced GPS technology, Grace has narrowed down the potential area to one of several abandoned temples in this region. Unfortunately, we don't know if they're holding all the material in that single location. Still, there also may be important information stored on systems inside the temple to assist with locating the remaining biohazards."

"Who did we piss off to get this duty?" Sam speaks softly to Cesar under his breath.

The commander gives Sam a scornful look as he walks over to power on the room projector. Not wanting to get any extra Kitchen Patrol duty, Sam sits upright and resumes listening quietly.

The projector fans hum lightly as it lights the screen at the front of the room. Grace flips her shoulder-length red ponytail toward her back and instinctively plugs her laptop into a loose video cable on top of the table. She clicks a pen next to her laptop and activates a green laser pointer. Making a circular motion on the screen with the laser, Grace begins speaking.

"Using proprietary tracking software I designed, I was able to identify the unique signature from the containers in the region. The last known, viable signal came from this abandoned town. I presume this temple is in the center of the town where we'll find either the biohazard or hopefully some computer systems I can hack into. Once I infiltrate their systems, I hope to learn where they may have stored the material, their objectives and help you stop them quickly."

As her information briefing trails off, the commander continues where she left off.

"Grace is a white hat hacker and encryption specialist. She will acquire any information on the biological weapon stolen from their corporation and the whereabouts of this terrorist cell."

The commander looks over at Dominik with a tense stare and in a terse tone, says,

"They will then share that intel with the military so that we can deal with that threat."

Eric, inquisitively, leans forward across the table toward Grace and asks,

"What can you tell us about the biohazard?"

Grace leans back in her seat and folds her arms in a ploy to evade the answer and states,

"I'm afraid I can't tell you much, except it's proprietary and catastrophically dangerous in the wrong hands."

Eric stares at Grace for a moment. Then, agitated by Grace's answer, he leans back into his chair while expressing his dislike for the assignment.

"Colonel, am I understanding this correctly? These rich corporate *yahoos* lost their dangerous experiment; now my team has to be their personal Uber ride and babysitter?"

The Colonel leans forward and scowls as he addresses Eric's comment.

"You will be a babysitter or whatever if that's what you are ordered to do, Sergeant."

Dominik speaks to address Eric's comment.

"What is the name of your squad again?" He thinks, "Ah yes... Hell Hounds. Sergeant, your special forces team is best suited to assist with recovering our property."

Dominik walks over and attempts to pat Grace's shoulder again as he continues speaking,

"Not withstanding your obvious disdain for the rich, I'm still entrusting you with my best employee; she's like a daughter to me."

Even more annoyed by Dominik's overt attention, Grace quickly slumps in the chair and then drops her shoulder out of reach of his hand. At that moment, Eric caught a quick glimpse of the ring on Dominik's right hand. Not that it stood out, but it contained a Christian-like symbol Eric had never seen before. The center of Dominik's ring was black onyx with a red cross on the left side and a hook that resembled a wide, lower case "h" attached to the lower part of the cross.

Again, Dominik continues speaking as if he didn't notice Grace's movements.

"Besides, if you're successful, our company will be deeply indebted to the US mili..."

Grace quickly interjects herself, cutting off Dominik and closing her laptop lid.

"This wouldn't be babysitting, Sergeant. I have had four weeks of intense desert survival training to prepare for this mission. I'm not a child; I'm capable of handling myself."

Eric unfolds his arms and stands up. Leaning over the table in front of Grace, he places his hands on the table as he looks her in the eye. He begins to raise his voice as he speaks with a condescending confrontational tone.

"Well, *la de dah...survival training* at the community *YMCA*. Look, *Princess Ariel,* this is going to get dangerous, and people who are unprepared die every day. I'm NOT going to be responsible for you!"

Undeterred by Eric's aggressive tactic, Grace stands up and raises her voice.

"First, Sergeant *big brother,* let's get one thing straight. My name isn't Ariel. It's Grace. Second, innocent people need our help. If you do your job and get me inside the temple, I'll do mine and get the biohazard or the intel!"

The strength of her conviction caught Eric off guard. Dominik smiles to attempt to defuse the conversation then adds,

"Sergeant, in my opinion, she's as proficient at her job as she is stubborn. I assure you, she's a gifted young woman, sometimes it's almost like she can read others' minds."

The Colonel, upset at Eric's tactics, also interjects by barking orders to the squad cutting off Eric's opportunity to respond.

"Stagg and Dragon will be your pilots. They will *Uber* your squad to the determined drop-off point....dismissed!"

The sound of chairs sliding back at once fills the conference room as the squad begins to exit the conference room. The Colonel walks out of the conference room and into the hallway, immediately behind Eric as he leaves. He orders Eric to wait then lowers his voice so that no one else in the hallway can hear.

"Global Unity is the largest military supplier. They've promised the government significant discounts for future purchases if we play ball. Seems a little odd, and not to mention that your squad was specifically requested to handle this."

The Colonel positions himself closer to Eric and continues to speak using what is commonly referred to as the "knife hand" gesture into Eric's chest.

"Retrieve this biohazard, bring the girl back in one piece. And please don't pull any of that movie, video game hero bullshit out there. Do I make myself clear?"

Eric doesn't like it, but he knows he doesn't have a choice. He looks intently back into the commanding officer's eyes,

"Crystal...Colonel."

The Colonel turns and begins to walk back towards the conference room door. Right before he entered, he turned to face Eric and slowly mouthed the words,

"One...piece!"

CHAPTER III

EARLY RISERS

Two days have passed since the team's initial briefing. Eric spent that time reviewing maps of the area and creating alternative strategies for quietly slipping in and out of the abandoned temple used by terrorists. On the third day, after his morning run, stopping the alarm after getting out of the shower, he makes his routine visit to the mess hall for coffee.

He takes his usual mental notes of the mess hall arrangement; pre-packaged breakfast sandwiches, juice dispenser, and then the coffee machine. Knowing that he was shortly going to be deployed on a mission made the pleasure of drinking a hot cup of brew alone more enjoyable. Eric leans on the usual table, allowing himself to relax in his routine. He glances off to his right to check the long tables where soldiers ate their meals. Everything was in order and as it had been every day since he had arrived. Until he glanced further down the dining hall where two soldiers were seated together talking near the middle of the room, they seemed familiar but somehow out of place from the usual bunch of early morning coffee drinkers.

The two soldiers' backs were turned toward Eric. They were obviously up to something, as they appeared to be speaking low as if they didn't want anyone to hear. Eric walks over to investigate; he tries to get close enough to listen to their conversation. Then, he would decide on any action he might need to take from there. Slowly he approached and was now close enough to hear their conversation. A familiar voice spoke softly.

"Man, where I'm from, all the nerds were ugly geeks.'

Eric relaxed when he was close enough and realized that the hushed tones were those of Sam and Darryl. Their proximity as they spoke was unusual for these two. He spoke loud enough for the two of them to hear.

"Sam, Darryl, what's up?"

Their reaction was evidence that Eric's voice slightly startled them. Not receiving an answer, he continued questioning.

"Are you boys up early for our training? It's not like either of you to let someone sneak up on you."

"Um, nothing, Sarg. We're just having our morning coffee," stated Sam nervously.

Their behavior became suspicious when they glanced down at the table and noticed they didn't have coffee cups. Eric pauses to glance in the direction of their gaze. That's when he sees Grace sitting at a table alone, coffee in hand. The table is piled high with manila folders, papers, and her laptop. Eric was impressed; she's been getting up early every day since her arrival here. Working in the mess hall made sense, especially since the barracks were small and drab. Not much incentive to spread out and work comfortably.

Grace's shoulder-length red hair was unbraided and appeared slightly wet. To Eric, she somehow seemed more youthful and vulnerable than the rigid computer hacker he met two days earlier. Holding her cup of coffee in one hand, she grabs a pen then scribbles some notes with her left hand. She crosses her legs then leans forward to peer onto her laptop screen. As she does this, her hair bristles into her face. She slowly pushes the hair out of her face, then behind her ear. She proceeds to spread out stacks of documents across the table. She was oblivious to the two rascals a few tables over.

Darryl glances back to Grace before leaning in close to Sam and quietly says,

"They didn't make computer nerds like that when a brother was in high school."

In a whispered voice, Sam speaks to Darryl.

"She's like the community librarian. You know it's bad to find her attractive, but somehow knowing that just makes her more attractive."

Eric interrupts their surprisingly garish behavior.

"C'mon, guys; she's *only* 22 or something. She could be our kid sister."

Darryl immediately shoots back at Eric's comment.

"She definitely can't be my kid sister."

Sam and Darryl fist bump as they laugh.

Eric studies Grace as she works. He starts to walk over to her table to amend their first meeting. Having had enough of Darryl and Sam's boyish antics, he decides that he and Grace may have gotten off on the wrong foot.

Seeing the sticker again on Grace's laptop, Eric felt that the game might be a bridge to start building a rapport. Then, a phrase from the game returns to his memory. As he approaches Grace's table, he proudly recites the phrase aloud.

"Gun down all the evil Gorgon enemies!"

Grace looks up, blinks several times rapidly, annoyed that someone broke her concentration, looking confused says,

"What?"

Eric attempts to recover from his embarrassing attempt to

appear young and hip. He points at the sticker on her laptop.

"I noticed the sticker. *Covert Wars*, right? I spent many nights battling inter-dimensional demons and other forces of evil in that game. I've finished the game in single battle mode."

Grace, unimpressed by Eric's gaming victory, begins to explain how the game is currently played.

"That's now considered the classic version of the game. If you choose, in the new version, you can play the dimensional demons attacking the military. The game is more realistic that way. There's no good and evil, just both sides attempting to survive."

She absent-mindedly looks down toward her laptop, ignoring Eric.

Eric turns around and spies Darryl shaking his head and covering his face. Sam begins laughing at his leader's great failure.

Eric, who had taken down several insurgents and led people into battle, was losing ground to a college-aged computer hacker. Feeling the urge to salvage what little dignity he had left, Eric states to Grace,

"I wanted to see how things were coming along on your end. I need to ensure you'll be ready."

Grace continued her work and never looked up. Not knowing what to do, abruptly, Eric turns and rigidly walks back to the table where Darryl and Sam were laughing. When he nears the table, Eric deepens his voice as he approaches the two misfits. Eric states sternly,

"Since you guys are up early, having fun, field rehearsals have been moved up 30 minutes."

He turns and walks away before the duo could protest.

CHAPTER IV

CONSPIRACY THEORIES

Eric arrives at the gun range 30 minutes early. He finds the team setup for the next round field rehearsal as ordered. He begins to set up his equipment; as he sets up, Eric starts to think about how lucky he was to find himself team leader of such a great group of misfits. He glanced over at Sam, an outstanding marksman and their field explosives expert.

Sam had once told Eric the story of how he joined the military. He grew up in a small mining town in mid-state California. His father worked mining rare earth metals. His dad often brought back a tiny number of dynamite caps and nitroglycerin used at the mine. At 17, he was arrested for exploding nitroglycerin with his brother. The story goes that he and his brother would fill bottles with nitro, then take them out to the canyons to shoot with guns and watch the bottles explode. One day, while out on one of these boyish adventures, his younger brother was setting up the bottles for their next round of shooting. Sam thought it would be funny to shoot one of the bottles near his brother and scare him. The problem was that the one bottle Sam hit was filled with extra nitro. Sam's little brother was too close when he shot the bottle. The blast sent Sam's little brother to the hospital unconscious, and Sam was held in custody overnight to teach him a lesson. His dad forced him to join the military as soon as he turned 18 to learn some discipline. Sam knew the hard way to respect explosives.

Another member of The Hell Hounds, Cesar, is in charge of communications and is also a serious Catholic. He will throw an "It's the will of God" statement into any situation. Cesar grew up in East Los Angeles in a neighborhood where gangs were prevalent. Cesar vowed that if he lived to see his eighteenth birthday, he would join the military to serve his country and leave the "barrio," as it was called within his Latin community.

Darryl, the third member of the group, was a light-hearted guy who consistently made jokes about the other guys. But that's how you knew he liked you. Darryl is also the team's conspiracy expert. Somehow, he always knew which celebrities sold their soul for fame or the latest government alien invasion cover-ups.

With his equipment set up, Eric decides to lighten the mood and make up for his harshness from earlier with some friendly shooting competition. He gets into position and fires downrange at the target. He overtly boasts to the others about his accuracy.

"Look at that grouping, boys. I've got a round of beers that says no one could beat my score."

Sam approaches the line.

"I'll take that bet!"

He draws his weapon and fires. The bullet goes through the chest portion of the target.

Darryl, gleefully surprised at Sam's accuracy for his first shot, shouts out,

"Ouch, that's gotta hurt Eric!"

Sam waits for everyone to settle down, takes a deep breath, relaxes his fingers on the trigger, pauses, and then lightly squeezes the trigger. The bullet pierces the head of the target. Darryl, unable to contain his excitement, shouts out again.

"Whoah!"

Sam playfully mocks Eric by proudly saying,

"Save your next paycheck Sarg; I'm going to be real thirsty after our next mission."

After the shooting exercise, the team stood around drinking water and talking for a bit. Then, with free beer on their minds, everyone started to loosen up and become talkative. Darryl starts the conversation by engaging the team in one of his recent conspiracy theories.

"You know the government has been injecting babies with alien DNA to develop superior humans."

Everyone starts to groan in disbelief. Darryl holds out his hand to pause his doubting audience.

"Hold on…This time, a brother has proof."

Darryl points to Eric and confidently begins his talk.

"Take Eric, for example; he's a good-looking, smart, former football player, self-defense expert, and marksman. No way, he got all that naturally. He had to be injected with alien DNA. You feel me?"

Everyone starts laughing heartily. They begin to elbow Darryl jokingly. His stories were usually whacky, but injecting babies with alien DNA, and I'm *one* of the babies? Eric is surprised to suddenly find himself as the core evidence of one of Darryl's nut job theories. C'mon! Eric thought to himself and then proudly spoke to the team. "Sorry to blow up your alien DNA theory about why I'm one of the best, but I was conceived naturally, born the old-fashioned way, and raised on a farm with a strict dad and loving mom."

The team enjoyed ribbing Darryl even more regarding his conspiracy theory about Eric being an alien love child. After that, they ran through the mock mission once again to regain their focus. Finally, after discussing locking down potential buildings that could be used as cover, they packed up their guns and equipment for the day.

CHAPTER V

THE MISSION

On the morning of the mission, Eric conducts the final briefing with Darryl, Sam, and Cesar. Dominik and Grace are also present. They review potential approaches and exits to the town. Finally, they agree upon an all-clear signal for the Stagg and Dragon to rendezvous and pick up the team.

Eric brings up a satellite photo of the site.

"The site looks abandoned, but you can never be sure. We are going in weapons hot - small packs only. Sam, there shouldn't be any need for explosives."

Sam nods his head in agreement.

"I need everyone to stay sharp. The goal is simple; Get Grace in, protect her while she packages or extracts data, and then get out safely. Everyone got that?"

Cesar asks everyone who's going on the mission to get in a circle and hold hands. Finally, he ends the meeting with a brief prayer.

"Lord, watch over us on our mission. And if anyone tries to stop us, forgive us for helping you fill up heaven."

Standing off to the side during the prayer, Dominik proceeds to walk over towards Eric. As he comes near, Eric notices that Dominik is wearing another dark blue tailor-made suit. He's also wearing a pin bearing that same cross-like symbol. Dominik begins speaking as he approaches Eric.

"Good luck Sergeant. Bring everyone home safe."

"Thank you, Dominik."

Eric takes a closer look at Dominik's pin on his suit and is puzzled by it.

"I meant to ask earlier, what is that cross symbol on your pin? I noticed it was also on your ring back in the conference room. Is that some new form of the Christian religion?"

Dominik replies,

"A new form of religion? No, Sergeant, not at all. It's much older. One that has existed for many more thousands of years."

After the meeting ends, everyone, except Darryl, heads back to gather their remaining equipment for the long helicopter ride to the drop-off point. Darryl approaches Eric and pulls him off to the side.

Darryl speaks quietly to Eric, "Something is weird with this mission, Sarge. Since when do we escort civilians into enemy territory?"

Eric leans into Darryl,

"Never. That's why I want you to stay next to her and keep an eye on our six," states Eric.

An hour later, Eric arrives at the helicopter airfield with his gear in hand. As Eric approaches the helicopter, he lets his bag drop to the ground to greet pilots Stagg and Dragon with a light fist bump.

"Just another day, Sarge," Stagg yells over the whirring of the blades. Eric smiles as he steps onto the chopper.

Grace is already on board, staring into her laptop screen as usual. Eric can see the light of the screen reflecting onto her face. Then Grace reviews the items she has in her backpack. She pulls out a rugged Pelican case that Eric assumes is for her laptop. She doesn't appear to notice Eric as he boards.

Sam, Cesar, and Darryl board the helicopter soon afterward. They're outfitted in military beige camouflage gear, Kevlar vest, laser scopes, and short-range communication headsets. Eric greets his team as they board with exploding fist bumps. He then sits down; he can see the pilots running through their final safety checks from his seat. He looks intensely at Grace as if peering inside her to see if she has what it takes to survive. In his hands were a pair of goggles. He motions to Grace to look in his direction as he begins to speak loud enough to be heard,

"These are night-vision goggles; they function as electronic eyes that boost weak night-time light into something more powerful. So basically, we can see in the dark. You're not getting a pair."

Motioning to his headset, Eric continues,

"This is a short-range communication device. We can speak to each other in a low voice and still hear clearly. You're not getting this either. Therefore, you'll need to follow my directions *to the letter,* or I cannot guarantee your safety. This is not virtual reality; if something goes wrong, people die. There's no reset. No do-over."

As the copter begins to lift, Grace yells over the whirring of the helicopter blades,

"I understand. I'm ready."

The copter lands outside of the town. The Hell Hounds team dismounts and stealthily walks toward the city that surrounds the temple. Eric is in front of the group, Cesar and Sam on each side of Grace; Darryl brings up the rear slightly behind the trio.

The desert night was still; the air was warm and dry; clouds hid the moon. Eric could barely see his hand in front of his face. The perfect cover for the team; hopefully, we can slip in and get out quietly, Eric thought to himself.

As they get closer to the edge of the village, Eric crouches and signals to the team to hold their position behind him. Viewing the area through his night-vision goggles gave Eric a highlighted, green-tinted view of his surroundings. Walking closer to the village, slightly ahead of the team, Eric's firearms were tightly pressed against his shoulder. He first scouts the terrain, then releases a single lens night vision binocular from his belt. Slowly removing his goggles, he presses the binocular to his right eye. As he peers into the distance, he sees one path that leads to the temple. It seemed to be about a half-mile from the edge of town to the temple.

Eric puts his night-vision goggles back on and turns back toward his team, holds up three fingers, and points to the ground nearest him. Crouching, Cesar starts to walk, Sam motions for Grace to proceed, and he follows behind her, periodically glancing behind him as they cautiously move towards Eric's location.

When the team reaches his location, Eric latches his binocular to his belt and signals for the team to proceed toward the first shanty building. Stealthily walking into the edge of the town, Eric reaches the first building, and the others arrive moments behind him. Shanty buildings on each side flank the path to the temple. Their approach appears to be intentionally impeded by debris stacked as high as the shanty buildings in various places. Although Eric knows combatants most likely are hiding in the buildings, he knows he and his team do not have time to search and clear each one.

Eric raises his gun to his shoulder and glances around the corner. He looks at Cesar; Cesar nods and raises his rifle to his shoulder, covering Eric's advance. Eric crouches and darts to the next building. Eric again signals for the team to proceed.

Using the abandoned, dilapidated buildings as cover, the

Hounds crisscross from one building to another as they make their way towards the main temple. On their third attempt at crossing the sandy path, bringing up the rear, Darryl hears the sound of wind above his head. He looks up to catch a glimpse of the rear outline of a massively sized animal leaping across the buildings over his head.

"Did you see that?" Darryl said over the communication devices.

"We aren't seeing anything," Eric replies.

What was that? Bears don't leap across buildings. Must've been the wind blowing a sheet or something." Darryl thinks to himself.

"Nothing," Darryl says into the comms.

Darryl's ear catches the faint sound of a cloth flap and light footsteps pressing against the sand. Out from the shadows, a figure appears. Brandishing a large blade, the figure advances quickly toward Darryl from the rear of the building. Darryl turns and through his night vision goggles, spots the figure approaching, focuses his M16 on the target, and instinctively releases two shots. The assailant's body jerks with each bullet impact to the chest. The dark figure took his last breath before his body met the sand-covered earth.

Eric, wondering why Darryl was delayed, decides to investigate. He heads back across the path to Darryl's last location. When he arrives, he finds Darryl standing over a downed hooded figure. In his right hand, the assailant was still clutching a blade with an engraved symbol. Eric removes his night vision goggles to get a better look at the corpse. Eric pulls a small LED flashlight from his belt. He reaches down and grabs the corpse's hood. Eric uncovers the face, revealing a young man, covered in white clay, lips covered in black chalk, and other dark markings around the cheeks. Uncovering the forearms, they discover more tattooed symbols, one of which seemed vaguely familiar to Eric. Realizing his time constraints, Eric planted this observation in the back of his mind to revisit later.

"Are those markings supposed to resemble a skull? This doesn't seem like Al Qaeda," says Darryl.

"Nah, it's some other type of religious nut. Keep your eyes open. This is a trap. We need to know what kind." Eric responds.

Eric and Darryl regroup with the team crouching behind a building. "Are we good?" asks Sam.

"Yes, stay tight. The next path that we cross has limited debris, which puts us out in the open," Eric tells his team.

Everyone nods. Eric looks at Grace. Remembering Eric's instructions on the helicopter, she also nodded even though she didn't quite understand what was going on.

When Eric decides the path is clear to continue, he steps out from the side of the building into the open. As he reaches the center of the path, another hooded figure, brandishing a sword in one hand, darts out from a dilapidated adobe building and charges toward Eric. As the assailant gets closer, he starts swinging his sword in a criss-cross pattern in front of his chest. As the attacker draws near, Grace wonders why Eric is just standing there. She can hear her frantic thoughts racing through her mind as she tries not to be afraid; he's just standing there. Why doesn't he shoot? Grace thinks to herself.

Eric's attacker comes near and attempts to bring his sword down onto Eric's chest. Eric releases his M16 from his grip, quick steps to one side, easily avoiding the deadly weapon. He then grabs the attacker's wrist that was holding the sword and uses his foe's momentum to force the robed figure to the ground. Eric then swiftly rolls himself backward on top of his attacker, pinning him down. He takes his handgun outfitted with a silencer from its holster and places a single shot into the hood.

Eric drags the body over to the nearest shadow, checks to see whether any zealots were hiding nearby, and gives a hand signal for the team to move to his position.

"C'mon Grace...move!" Sam abruptly exclaims.

It happened so fast Grace wasn't sure if she closed her eyes. After Eric's show of effortless combat skill against his attacker, the team continued to traverse the dwellings unabated for a while. Eric estimated that they were only thirty or so yards from the temple. Eric cautiously steps out on the path, raises his hand, and clenches his fist, signaling the team to hold their current position. He could tell the temple was in front of him but realized something wasn't right. It was too quiet. They were on a narrow street with tall dwellings on each side, and piles of what he assumed were strategically placed debris that blocked an otherwise easy advance to the temple entrance.

Eric returns to the team's position.

"Stop saying my name!" Grace frantically covers her ears.

"We're right here. No one is calling you," says Sam, urging her to be quiet.

"Yes, I can hear them. They are saying that they are waiting for me behind the debris wall," retorted Grace.

Darryl gives Eric a concerned look. Concerned but wanting to keep on the mission, Eric speaks in a hushed voice,

"Sam, try to calm Grace down. I think all this combat is sending her into some emotional shock. I'll go scout the area first. Get her back to the rendezvous point if I don't return. That's an order!"

CHAPTER VI

MAN AGAINST BEAST

Eric heads out alone into the darkness once again to scout the area. He knew the enemy would use the debris wall to hide behind. He passed between two tall debris walls blocking his view of his team. He looks at the nearby dwellings and surrounding area and realizes that they are walking into a kill zone. He could somehow feel the attackers watching from the shadows.

As he pauses to assess the location, he notices the head of a giant beast slowly start to peer out of the shadow in front of him. Lifting his goggles, giving his eyes a second to adjust, he realized the animal wasn't a dog. Despite the darkness, he could see the beast only had one large eye and a massive mane of hair like a lion behind its head. It snarled at Eric as it walked out of the shadows. As it approached, he could see saliva dripping off its large fangs. Whatever type of beast this was, Eric sensed it was hungry for his blood, and a bloodthirsty animal is always dangerous. Nevertheless, it continued to step out from the shadows to approach him.

He had never seen anything like this. Its height was level with Eric's shoulders. Its neck appeared to be too long to balance that colossal head. The beast growled threateningly at Eric and started shaking its head back and forth, its mane swaying back and forth as it did so. Saliva was dripping from its mouth as it growled more menacingly. It was the weirdest creature Eric had ever seen. "Was the creature a result of the corporation's bioweapon?" he thought. Eric raised his weapon in an attempt to ward off the creature. As he raised his gun, the beast let out an intense growl that Eric swore he could feel. At the same time, the beast's large mane, tail fur, and eyes started to glow intensely red like a burning flame. At that moment, the beast charged and leaped menacingly toward Eric.

Seeing the animal's mane and eye change color was unbelievable. It shocked him so much he was caught off guard as the beast attacked. Its jaws open, sharp teeth protruding as it lunged toward Eric. Although Eric's training instinctively took over, he stammered back, barely adjusting his shoulder out of the way of the beast's vicious bite. Unfortunately, the beast landed on Eric with enough force to knock him to the ground

As the beast stood over him, it attempted to bite down on Eric again, but he held his M16 in both hands across his chest. The beast's jaws locked on the weapon instead of Eric's flesh. With the gun in its jaws, the beast shook its head violently from side to side in an attempt to loosen Eric's grip on the rifle.

"Sarge, what's the holdup?" Eric could hear Sam over his comms. He briefly turned to see if the others were watching, but he couldn't see them from their holding position.

Eric could feel the hot, sulfur-smelling breath of the beast as it continued to shake loose his weapon. Eric knew if he lost his weapon, he was as good as dead. His muscles strained under the force, but with a few more shakes, the beast loosened Eric's grip, and his M16 was tossed a few feet away. As the beast focused on Eric, its flame-colored hair intensified in color; then the beast, satisfied it had won, stood over Eric proudly. To add a final insult to its victory, it lowered its nose close to Eric's face. It then let its saliva slowly drip down onto Eric's face, as Eric's heart began frantically beating against his chest.

"Sarge, we're leaving our holding positions to find out what's going on," said Sam over comms.

Eric knew the team would be in a vulnerable position if he couldn't help himself. As the beast paused to savor its victory, Eric desperately reached around for something to defend himself with. As he reached around, his desperate fingertips found a long piece of wooden debris. The beast's head started to rise away from Eric's face. Eric grabbed the piece of wood and shoved toward the beast with all the energy his muscles could spare. The beast yelps in pain as the wooden stick meets its flesh.

The beast fell onto its hind legs in pain. Eric realized he stabbed the creature in its only eye. Instinctively, Eric rolls away from the beast, scrambles toward his weapon, and fires point-blank again and again at its muscular body. The beast fell to the ground, its flaming red hair dims and nearly goes out, but, then getting to its feet, it raises once more. Then, with blood still dripping from its eye socket, it moves its head to the left and right, sniffing the air as if to locate Eric's position.

"Ah, give up already!" Breathing heavy, Eric says to himself. His muscles ached as he wondered how such a creature was still alive.

The beast turns towards Eric and growls as it prepares to charge again. Eric could barely move; his muscles ached under the strain of fighting the beast, but instead of charging as Eric expected, the beast sniffed the air a second time, turned, and ran off.

Through the small opening between the two piles of debris, Eric could now see his team leaving their position behind the building approaching his location. As Eric anticipated, robed figures left their hiding spots. Brandishing blades and swords, the zealots started unleashing screams and howls as they attempted to ambush Eric's team.

The Hounds unleashed a hail of bullets in the direction of each of the rushing zealots, cutting them down like blades of grass through a mower as they charged. Grace's heart started pumping wildly with adrenaline as she covered her ears and fell to her knees to escape the sound of gun fire. The sound of the screaming and bodies hitting the ground from all directions was frightening her.

Eric attempts to shake off the shock to help his team, but his muscles are too tired to move after battling that beast.

An attacker leaps off one dwelling, knocking Cesar and Darryl to the ground simultaneously. The attacker then crawls on top of Darryl. Being caught off guard, he uses his gun to block the attacker's arms from forcing the knife into his throat. Blood pours from Cesar's cheek as he barely deflects the assailant's blade from slicing his throat open. Using the struggle as a distraction, a second attacker runs toward the team from the side of a dwelling, grabs Grace, and drags her away from the group.

"Shit, should I help Darryl or go after Grace?" Sam thinks, surprised they were caught off guard so quickly.

Hearing Grace's cry for help, adrenaline rushes through Eric's aching body. He jumps to his feet and darts between the debris walls to better view the skirmish. He doesn't like what he sees; he raises his weapon and, in one motion, fires a bullet at Darryl's attacker's hood. The zealot's brain shortly exits the hood after the bullet leaves his skull. Seeing this, most of the remaining zealots flee the area.

Eric walks over to where Darryl is laying on the ground.

"This your final resting place?" Speaking sharply to Darryl.

Although Darryl's face is bleeding, he snaps back,

"No sir, a brother isn't dying tonight," Darryl said with conviction.

Eric reaches out his hand. Darryl grabs it, and Eric pulls him up. While Darryl stands, Cesar hears something to his left, turns and fires at another charging assailant. Darryl stands erect, and Eric nods to him.

"Wait here, I'm going to get Grace," Eric tells the team.

He finds the trail left from Grace being dragged away through his night-vision goggles. He follows it into a dilapidated, abandoned building. Eric can see the guy punching Grace and attempting to rip off her clothes. As he attempts to rape her, Eric has a flashback to his younger sister that he failed to protect when he was younger. He angrily grabs the attempted rapist by his hood and jerks him backward off of Grace and onto the floor. Eric jabs his knee into his chest and punches him in the face. The zealot tries to reach for his knife.

"He's going for his knife!" Grace yelled.

This is what Eric was waiting for. As the zealot swings his knife, Eric leaps up and off his chest, releases his handgun from its clip, draws the weapon, and shoots the guys in the balls. Just as the pain of being shot reaches his brain, Eric squeezes off two shots, close range into his forehead.

Eric turns toward Grace, who is trembling and crying. He reaches out his hand to her. Grace wipes her tears, nods, then reaches out for his hand. Eric noticed that her hand was soft and trembling, almost like a child.

"Take his knife as a reminder to never let anyone threaten you again," Eric tells Grace.

Grace reaches down, grabs her backpack and the knife he used to attack her, then kicks the rapist zealot in the side. Eric smiles,

"Atta girl," Eric says approvingly.

"From now on, hold on to my belt; when I move, you move. I'll know immediately if something happens to you."

They stealthily head back to rendezvous with the other Hounds still in defensive formation.

CHAPTER VII

THE TEMPLE

After successfully defending against the zealot ambush, the team continues unabated until reaching the temple entrance. They scramble for cover inside the main temple hall. Attempting to surprise the Hounds, a knife-yielding zealot yells as he drops from the ceiling; Sam turns and places a clean shot to the chest. Still, in mid-air, the zealot is knocked backward through a weak wall revealing a small room with surprisingly sophisticated computers and communication equipment.

"*Looka'* here at the fancy stuff these wanna-be Al Qaeda purchased on Eastbay's website," said Sam.

Eric walks over to the hooded body on the floor. Stands over the body and once more removes the hood covering a face covered in white and black clay.

"Grace, you're up; get whatever information you need before these hooded freaks bring reinforcements." Eric orders.

Grace hurries through the tattered opening and scrambles to assemble her laptop and equipment on the table. She connects her computer to one of the systems on the table; force reboots their computer, then starts to type a command, *ren utilman.exe.*

Eric watches for a moment before asking her,

"I had a run-in with a creature I can't explain. Does that bioweapon turn animals into insane-looking, one-eyed creatures?"

"Sorry, Eric, but that is proprietary information," Grace states matter-of-factly.

Not happy with that answer, Eric turns his attention back to his team.

"Sam, Cesar, guard the windows. Shoot anything that moves. I don't care if it's a wandering emu!" Eric barks.

The team moves to occupy the windows while Grace works. After 20 minutes, Grace stands up from the chair, starts packing up her equipment, then hands Eric a USB drive.

"This is the information for the Colonel," said Grace.

Eric looks at her, surprised, not wanting to look too impressed.

"Dominik said you were good. Was it really that easy?" Eric asks.

"They were using Windows. I rebooted the system, used my system to offline reset their admin password, then I typed..." Grace starts to explain.

Eric cuts her off by holding up his hand.

"One day, I hope to have the time to understand what you were trying to explain, but tonight is not it!" states Eric.

Eric hands the drive back to Grace, and she places it into her pack. He walks back through the broken wall, puts his back to the wall, and peers out the door to size up the situation. Everything appears quiet. Eric knows that reinforcements are on the way, and if he were in their shoes, they would be planning to storm the temple.

Grace reaches into her pack and pulls out a first aid kit. She takes out gauze and tape.

"Sit down, Cesar," Grace says maternally.

As Cesar sits down, Grace starts to apply ointment to his face.

"This scar will be the best pickup conversation starter," Darryl slightly chuckles.

Eric looks back at Cesar's bleeding face and then to Grace, who is afraid, but composed.

"Sam, set C4 to blow this place back to the seventh heaven or wherever they go when they die," Eric orders.

"Yes, sir, this place will light up like Christmas on the fourth of July!" Sam jokes sarcastically.

"Hounds, let's show these religious nuts why you don't bring a knife to a gunfight!" Eric states emphatically.

Cesar and Sam smile.

"Lock and load Hell Hounds!" Darryl barks.

Sam begins to place explosives around the room on the temple walls. He wires a single timer. The timer shows 10 minutes. Sam nods to Eric.

"Grace, you're with me," Eric orders.

Grace walks over to Eric and stands behind him, placing her hand on his belt. Eric drops his night vision goggles over his face, positions his gun to his shoulder, and fires out the door into the night. Grace holds Eric's belt and follows him out next to Sam. Lastly, Cesar steps through the door, followed by Darryl.

Having walked the street already, the Hell Hounds were sharp and prepared. As they walked back through the town, they picked up their pace. Sam's watch begins to beep.

"Call them out as you see them," Eric orders.

The team stops, removes their night vision goggles, and kneels, keeping their guns focused as they scan the surrounding area. Then, as the explosives blow the temple to pieces, the street is lit up like daylight for a few moments, revealing startled zealot attackers. They suddenly lose their cover as their eyes adjust to the light from the exploding temple.

"My 11, 12, and 2," Eric calls out.

Attackers charging Eric with swords drawn were startled by the explosion; they paused, realizing their nighttime advantage had been lost. Three effortless squeezes on the trigger by Eric stopped the surprised attacker's hearts the moment the bullets entered their chests.

"Rooftop, 10 o'clock!" Sam calls out.

Sam softly squeezes the trigger as he watches the body jerk then drop.

"Doorway and window, my 3...now down," Cesar calls out.

The momentary explosion was the distraction needed to take out the attackers. Gunning them down quickly.

CHAPTER VIII

A NEW DAWN

The exhausted team sits on rocks in the sand-covered clearing. Cesar has a clean bandage over his cheek wound. The sun was starting to rise. They could hear the faint sound of a helicopter in the distance.

"Sam, set off a ground flare," says Eric.

Sam pops a flare and throws it to the ground. The team could now hear the helicopter change to the direction of the signal.

As the helicopter flies over the town to find a clear place to land, the pilot, Dragon, notices the small town littered with approximately 40-50 bloody bodies on rooftops, in the streets, and hanging out of windows. The copilot, Max, notices the charred temple and then speaks to the pilot over the comms in disbelief,

"Damn, they did all that damage?"

Finding a clear area, the helicopter hovers, allowing the Hell Hounds to quickly board.

"That's how they got their name. They're loyal, and they bring the fury of Hell itself to every mission," the pilot remarks over the comms.

The small-framed, female copilot leaves her seat to verify that the Hell Hounds are safely on board. Recognizing Eric as the team leader, she stares intently at him for a moment before returning back to her seat and assisting in guiding the copter away.

At the same moment, Eric sensed someone was looking at him and realized the copilot wasn't Stagg, his usual copilot. He catches a glimpse of her name tag before she returns to her seat. Through the haze of muscle aches and exhaustion, he could barely make it out. He only saw it briefly; it looked like "Max." Odd name for a woman pilot, he thought. Eric ponders why his usual copilot was subbed out without his input or approval. A discussion is to be brought up later once back at the base. For now, the only thing that mattered to him was that his team was safe and obtained their objective.

As Eric gazes at the back of Max's head, she notices this and quickly refocuses on the helicopter console.

Grace, tired and bruised, looks at Eric drifting off to sleep. She felt this was as good a time as any to ask the question that had been racking her brain before the mission. She leans towards Eric and quietly asks,

"Eric...One question?"

Eric pauses, looking in her direction with a tired gaze.

"Yes?"

"Who is Ariel?"

Exhaustion overcame Eric, and he fell asleep without answering.

The copter maneuvers in the direction of the base without a single trace of life in the town.

CHAPTER IX

GUN RANGE

After visiting the base doctors, and several days of physical therapy, Eric was glad to be medically cleared and able to get back to his morning run. He enjoyed getting up before most of the base awoke, and he especially enjoyed running in the morning before the desert sun began to rise.

As Eric jogged around the base, albeit at a slower pace, he realized what he truly loved about his morning run. What he truly loved was seeing the first hints of the sun's rays dance over the mountain tops or through the clouds. For a fleeting moment, it all made sense. Only for a brief moment did he feel connected to something more than himself. Through these moments, he gained the desire to live and fight to fulfill his desire to run with the dancing sun rays one more day. So today, Eric took a detour from his usual path. Approaching the east barracks, Eric takes a note from his pocket and checks the address on the door as he approaches.

Grace enjoyed sitting crossed-legged on her bed after waking early to work on her computer encryption projects. To her, decrypting hash were nothing but little puzzle pieces that only needed to be turned over or rotated correctly to get all the pieces in the right place in order to form the correct picture. She usually felt comfortable in her loosely fitting long white t-shirt, dark red tie-dyed leggings, and black socks to keep her feet warm as she worked. As she sat, she had papers and manila folders sprawled across her bed.

She becomes distracted when she notices a shadowy figure walking by her window. When there is a knock at the door, she immediately becomes nervous. Strange, why would someone be at my door at the crack of dawn? Do we have new information on the terrorist group? Grace ponders these thoughts to herself as she approaches the door. She opens the door slightly and peeks outside to find Eric standing there in fatigues and a white shirt.

As Eric suspected, Grace was already up and working. He steps closer to the door to ensure she knows it is him. When she realizes who it is, she relaxes and opens the door wider. Grace couldn't help but notice Eric's face was splotchy red with bruises.

"Let's go for a walk," Eric tells her.

"Did something happen?" Grace states, confused, peeking outside the door. The sun is just beginning to display its fiery morning light.

"Come with me. I have something I want to show you," Eric calmly states.

Grace, not sure what was going on, hesitantly nodded in agreement.

"Wait here. I need a minute to change," Grace told him.

Eric steps back, allowing her to close the door. She walks back to her bed and quickly gathers up her work, and place it underneath her bed. Grace removes her leggings and long t-shirt and then hops into the shower. Grabbing a bar of soap, she closes her eyes as she instinctively rubs the soap into a lather on her skin. Her mind begins to wander as she starts sizing up Eric. Eric's a bit overbearing and overprotective, but he has a good heart. She thought to herself.

As Eric stands outside, he begins to look at his watch, wondering how much longer he would need to wait for her to change clothes. Grace finally opened the door. She was wearing black jeans, heavy boots, a short sleeve blouse, and her red hair was down and slightly damp.

"Close your eyes and put your hands on my shoulders. I have a surprise waiting on you." Eric tells her.

She closed her eyes and held on tightly to Eric as he guided her on a long winding path around the barracks. This became uncomfortable as it reminded her of their mission. In her mind, she could hear Eric saying, hold on to me tightly. Grace began to squeeze Eric's shoulders tighter as images of the recent mission where she was captured, dragged away, and almost raped at the hand of some religious zealots began to play out in her mind.

"Open your eyes now," She could hear Eric say, snapping out of her brief trauma.

She became more confused when their walk ended at the shooting range; Grace glanced at Eric with a puzzled gaze. Eric leads her into the shooting range where he had previously dismantled a few handguns.

"I know you've probably had self-defense classes already, but I wanted to show you a different approach to defending yourself."

Eric picks up a gun.

"This is a Glock 19 millimeter. Watch carefully. I am going to show you how to assemble, load, and more importantly, unload it."

He then begins to explain each part. Afterward, he shows her how to assemble and load the gun. Eric allows Grace to demonstrate what she has just learned. He gives her an impressed look.

"Looks like you've got that part down. Now, let's get to the fun part of the training."

He shows her how to release the safety and aim the pistol. Eric hands the pistol to Grace. Holding the pistol toward the target, she squeezes the trigger and fires at the target, hitting the target in the hip section.

"You can let go of the trigger now," Eric states.

Grace didn't realize that she was still squeezing the trigger tightly.

"Hmm...Well, at least you're hitting the target." Eric states humorously. "Hold the gun secure but not too tight. Here, let me show you."

Eric slowly comes up behind Grace. Reaching for the gun, he puts his hand on top of hers. Placing his right shoulder against her shoulder allowed her to brace herself against him. He then put his other arm around her and stated,

"Square it up with your shoulder and then gently squeeze the trigger."

The next shot goes near the chest area. Eric releases his hand and steps back.

"Look at that! Anybody would be taken down with a shot like that."

Being excited about the growth she has made in such a short time, Grace throws her arms around Eric's neck. Knowing how to handle a firearm correctly gave her a sense of empowerment. Maybe Eric would allow her to carry one into the field on their next mission.

As Sam walks into the gun range, he sees Grace embrace Eric. Seeing this, he couldn't help but feel jealous and now wonders if he should mention what he saw to the other guys on the team.

"Why are you interested in helping me? "Grace asks Eric.

"I feel as though if I help you, if a situation arises, you can take care of yourself. I might get a second chance at saving someone," Eric states sadly.

CHAPTER X

THE WORM

Later that evening, Eric walks into the large tent used by the corporation to house their computer equipment and contractors. Several contractors are roaming about holding papers and talking to one another. Eric finds Grace intently staring at her screen. This wasn't unusual, but what *was* odd was that she seemed antsy. When Eric reached her desk, he noticed she was biting her nails and nervously bouncing her legs up and down.

"Grace, what's going on?" asked Eric.

"Shh, I am waiting," Grace said, trying to ignore Eric.

Grace, never looking away from the screen, starts biting her nails again. Eric is unable to hold off his question any longer.

"What are you waiting for?" Eric asked impatiently.

"Well, after I hacked into the computer system of those knife-wielding weirdos, I decided to try something. I sent out a broadcast email labeled, *Jessica Alba, Hot Must See*. If anyone opens the attachment, it will execute a *little* worm I coded."

"A worm? So what will this little worm do?" Eric asked, confused.

'The worm will run in stealth mode, gathering information about the network it's on. IP address, DNS and ARP information…." Grace proceeds to explain.

Eric holds up his hand in a motion to suggest she shouldn't bother to explain further, as the information was too technically complex for him.

Grace continues.

"Sorry. Well, anyway, the worm will compress all the data and make copies of itself onto every device connected to the network. Once one of the copies discovers an internet connection, the worm will encrypt that data and send it to me."

"I don't get the big deal. You'll know how many computers are on their network? So what, how does that help my team?" Eric asks.

"Simple, really. Most client systems have to keep time within 15 minutes of their server. Out of habit, most system administrators configure their servers with the time of their locale. I can cross-reference their network's time information with the time and location of the internet router the worm is connecting to," Grace says.

"Hmmm...Let's see; first, we have to rely on some guy being horny enough to open an attachment from an unknown sender. Second, we hope this worm can get to a system that eventually attaches to the internet. Third, even if all that happens, all we'll really have is a lot of random data that will need to be sifted through."

Eric pauses and looks briefly at Grace before continuing.

"This worm plan is based on a lot of hope, and frankly, hope is not a good plan, Grace. Besides, it's going to take too much time. I don't want to sit around waiting for a bunch of *geeks to sort* through a bunch of 1s and 0s," Eric states with a look of uncertainty.

Grace folds her arms and bites her bottom lip to ponder Eric's statement before responding.

"Another approach is, since the worms never stop broadcasting, one of the users may connect to an internet cafe a few times. Then, although there will be a slight delay, I can use the worm to trace-route their actual location.

Grace pauses for a split second, puts a smirk on her face, leans forward in her chair, and continues in a sharp tone.

"Then *you* and the *Hounds* can charge in, fire off a few rounds of ammo, blow the building up with explosives, and if possible, apprehend the suspect. That is if there is anything left *to* apprehend."

Eric's face lights up, and his eyes widen.

"I know you're being a smart ass, but seriously that is a great plan. Since that's all we've got to go on, that'll have to work for now. Let me know if any horny terrorist opens your attachment," Eric states contently.

As he turns to walk away from Grace, he starts shaking his head and laughs to himself quietly,

"What a smart ass...Blow the place up...Gotta love these crazy social media kids."

As he takes a step, he notices the Colonel hurriedly walking towards him.

"Eric, I need to speak with you immediately," The Colonel states.

Eric steps away from Grace's desk toward his commanding officer.

"What's up, commander?" Eric asked, puzzled.

In a low solemn voice, the Colonel responds,

"Eric, you're being charged with war crimes."

Eric drops his smile, replacing it with a devastated expression.

"War crimes? You must be joking." Then, not wanting to forget his rank, he adds, "Sir."

The Colonel tells Eric,

"There are witnesses. Look, I told them I wanted to tell you first."

Sensing his colonel's lack of humor, he instinctively peers up over the colonel's left shoulder toward the door just as two Military

Police officers step inside the room. They had their distinctive red and white MP band around their right arm.

The two MPs, Frick and Frack, nick names Eric had given the two officers due to their pompous attitudes, approach behind the commander.

"Sergeant Eric?" Asks Frick.

"What's this about?" Eric asks.

"Charges have been filed against you, sir. You're under arrest for war crimes," Frick states.

Shocked, Eric looks directly into Frick's eyes and angrily states, "This is crazy."

He walks past his commander and attempts to walk between the two MP Officers. The MPs immediately close the gap. He felt his hand clenching into a tight fist as the MPs blocked his exit. Eric notices Frack placing his hand on his gun and unfastens the holster clip. He could tell that Frack was slightly younger than Frick. Eric thought that Frack's inexperience would lead to a problem if he didn't remove his hand from his firearm. I could take them both down before he upholsters that firearm. Eric thought to himself.

Eric glances back towards Grace; he can see her slowly standing up. Her eyes have a look of concern as she covers her mouth with her hands. Her expression reminded him of how his little sister looked the night the police arrived at their home. This can't be happening again. Eric thought.

In an attempt to diffuse the growing hostility, the Colonel places his hand on Eric's shoulder and tells him,

"Eric, please relax. I'm going to see what I can find out, and I will vouch for your career and leadership."

The First MP pulls out a pair of handcuffs and steps towards Eric. Eric tenses his muscles, prepared to take on the two MPs.

The younger MP stares at Eric as time starts to slow down; he nervously clenches the holster of his gun, ready to engage. He wasn't confident Eric wouldn't lose his cool and challenge them. He didn't want to pull his gun in a room full of people, but he would if it came down to that.

The Commander waves off the MP and states,

"That won't be necessary. I'll ride along and ensure Eric makes it to the guardhouse."

A few hours later, as Eric sits in the holding cell, he starts reminiscing about the circumstances surrounding how he became a Marine.

CHAPTER XI

ERIC'S MILITARY BEGINNING

Eric had a strict but loving childhood. He grew up in an ordinary house in a small middle-class neighborhood. He had a sister, Laura, who was quiet and reserved. He attended the school in his community and was well-liked by peers. He had a strict father and a mother who adored them.

His father was honorably discharged from the military after he protected a black enlisted officer from abuse by white officers. He was well respected in the community and ran the local Veteran's counseling organization. The family owned a small farm and made enough money to make an honest living.

As far back as Eric could remember, his father raised him with military-like discipline. They were up to run every morning at 5:30 a.m. before he went to school. Eric would ask his dad why he still wakes up so early to work out. His dad would tell him, "Son, you can take the man out of the Corps, but you can't take the Corps out of the man."

When Eric was older, his dad would put sand in a backpack and have him run a few miles. His dad would add a little more sand each day to strengthen his endurance as he improved his time. On several occasions, Eric's dad would teach him self-defense moves and remind him it was his duty to protect those who couldn't protect themselves.

He remembered his dad always told him to be back home before dark while young and always in before midnight while in high school. He fondly remembers his dad being tough yet fair.

Eric knew everyone at his high school but only kept one close friend, Tom. Tom was brash and always bragging about himself. Eric and Tom were members of the football team. Although Eric played sports, he wasn't a dumb jock by any means. He was always one of the best students in class. He loved playing video strategy and sports games mostly. It was easy for him to develop a strategy to beat most games.

One night, when Eric's father was away speaking at a Veterans event, Eric, his best friend Tom and some teammates were at his house drinking. Tom became seriously intoxicated and decided he would go to Eric's sister's room and tell her how pretty he thought she was. Once Tom realized Eric had a lot to drink and wasn't paying attention, Tom slipped into Laura's room, grabbed her, and started to kiss her. She tried to fight back, but Tom, a football player, was too strong. He started to rip off Laura's clothes and began to grope her. Laura was screaming for Eric to help her, but then Tom slapped her on the face, covered her mouth, and told her,

"Lay still and be quiet."

Laura's face grimaces with pain.

When Eric came to, he could hear scuffling in his sister's room and realized Tom was missing. Eric burst into Laura's room with a wooden bat and started hitting Tom. Tom was knocked unconscious, and his sister grabbed Eric to stop him from hitting Tom. Blood dripped down the tip of the bat. Laura put on a jacket, ran downstairs, grabbed her mobile phone, and called the sheriff. The other teammates wondered what was going on as Laura rushed past them.

An ambulance arrived to take Tom to the hospital. Tom was now in a coma. The doctors weren't sure if he would be the same after he recovered. Eric had lost control.

The following week, the sheriff and deputy show up at Eric's house. They ask Eric's father to step outside to talk. When the sheriff began speaking, Eric's father immediately turned bloodshot red. Eric's father reluctantly called for Eric to come outside. He then explains to Eric that Tom's parents were filing charges against him for battery and attempted murder. The judge ordered him to be detained until the arraignment. Neighbors started to gather outside their homes to see what was going on. The police handcuff Eric and lead him to their car. As they walked him to the car, Eric hung his head low. He was now the talk of the small town.

Eric's dad came to visit him in the local jail. Eric's sister had hung herself. The pain of what happened to her was too much for her to bear.

"I failed, dad. I failed to protect someone who needed help," Eric said, in distress.

"Don't worry about that, son. Laura is in a better place now. We need to help you now."

Since he was previously a star athlete and a good student, before the trial began, Eric's dad asked the judge to allow Eric to join the military. Feeling that it was best not to ruin a promising life, the judge agrees.

The judge releases Eric on his word that he would join the military and make something good of his life. Eric knew the Marines did the most challenging work in the military. He decided to follow after his dad and desired to prove to his dad that he could be a better person.

CHAPTER XII

THE TRIAL

During the first day of the trial proceedings, Grace sits near the front of the room close to Eric. The Hell Hounds sit in the front row wearing their best uniforms for the trial. Dominik sits in the back of the room, observing the proceedings. He is wearing another blue custom suit and designer shades.

Eric, sitting at the defendant's table with his hands folded, is wearing his Service B uniform. Eric looks at his Judge Advocate Division (JAD) court-appointed counselor. He was good at sizing people, and he could tell this guy was nervous. He was so nervous he was almost sweating. Eric was beginning to think this guy was younger than him. Eric takes the opportunity to glance over at the prosecuting attorney. He is an older JAD officer, dressed in formal wear with a white jacket. He looks calm and confident as he reviews documents with his partner. Eric's JAD counselor is dressed in a Service B uniform as well.

Eric slowly leans over to his JAD counselor,

"Can you tell me how many cases you've tried again?"

Defense counselor,

"Well, I was top of my class in the Judge Advocate courses."

Eric got the distinct impression this may not be going in his favor. The bailiff begins to speak,

"All rise."

The judge sits down and begins the court session.

"United States vs. Sergeant Eric Lansing. Defense, call your first witness."

The Defense Counselor responds,

"Thank you. Your honor, I call Colonel Wells to the stand."

The defense waits for the colonel to approach the bench, get sworn in, and sit down.

"How many soldiers do you have under your command, Colonel?" The Defense Counselor asks.

Colonel Wells responds,

"Thousands at Camp Dwyer, but I don't interact with all of them. There are protocols in place for chains of command."

"Although you don't interact with everyone, is it safe to say you do have direct interaction with Sergeant Major Lansing?" Asks the Defense Counselor calmly.

"Yes, the Sergeant is assigned to a special team that reports directly to me," Replies Colonel Wells.

The Defense Counselor slowly walks towards the witness stand and asks,

"Colonel, how would you describe Sergeant Eric Lansing's leadership qualities?"

"Eric is a fine upstanding fire squad commander. A solid leader." Colonel Wells quickly responds.

"Thank you, Colonel. No more questions, your honor," said the Defense Counselor.

"Prosecution, your witness," said the Judge.

The prosecuting counselor stands, pulls down the bottom of his jacket to straighten his uniform as he approaches the witness stand. He then begins speaking to Colonel Wells,

"Colonel, thank you for being here today. I know you are very busy. In your earlier testimony, you stated that Sergeant Lansing is a solid leader. Is that correct?"

"Yes, that's right." Responds the Colonel.

The Prosecuting Counselor continues,

"Colonel, is it true that on several occasions Sergeant Lansing's cavalier approach to his special missions often put his team in unnecessary danger, and he had to be disciplined by you?"

"Yes, Eric is a special soldier. Occasionally, as his commander, I need to ensure protocol is followed." The Colonel responds.

The Prosecutor starts speaking at a quickening pace,

"Are you suggesting that Eric often doesn't follow military protocols?"

"Well, I am not exactly saying that. What I'm..." The Colonel responds defensively.

The Prosecutor interrupts the Colonel's testimony, catching him off guard, and fires back,

"Isn't it true that due to the sensitivity of his recent mission, you warned the Sergeant he was not to stray, as you stated earlier, away from military protocol?"

"Yes, but that's not exactly what I meant...." The Colonel responds, attempting to clarify his prior statement.

The Prosecutor cuts off the Colonel once again,

"Thank you, Colonel. No further questions, your honor."

The Prosecuting Counselor turns and quickly walks back to the prosecutor's table. The bailiff opens the witness stand door and waits for the Colonel to exit.

The Colonel remarks under his breath,

"What a bastard."

Day 2 of The Trial

Sam is called to the witness stand by the Prosecution. The Prosecuting Counselor approaches the witness stand to begin his questioning.

"Corporal, did Sergeant Lansing order you to blow up a sacred religious site or not?"

Sam, starting to feel pressure, nervously responds,

"It was an ambush! I don't know how they knew we would be there, but Sarge did what he could do to ensure everyone made it out safely."

The Prosecuting Counselor responds to Sam's emotional statement,

"A simple yes or no answer will suffice."

"Yes, but..." Sam attempts to respond, but the Prosecuting Counselor cuts him off.

"That will be all. You may step down now."

Day 3 of The Trial

Grace is called to the stand by the Prosecution. The Prosecutor begins his questioning,

"Grace, you were the lone civilian on this trip, correct?"

"Yes," Grace responds.

The Prosecuting Counselor continues,

"So, it was a part of Eric's Squad's mission to protect you?"

Again, Grace responds,

"Yes."

"Did you hear the sergeant tell his men to shoot anything that moves; Even helpless animals that may wander near the temple?"

Grace responds,

"Yes, he was attacked by some sort of wild animal. He was nearly passed out, and there were assassins everywhere."

The Prosecuting Counselor walks over to glance at his notes before resuming. He then retorts,

"Wild beasts and assassins everywhere? Sounds like a fanciful fairy tale. Did you see these religious assassins or wild beasts?"

He positions himself closer to Grace,

"Or, is this what the sergeant told you?"

Grace was starting to feel uncomfortable as the prosecutor positioned himself near her personal space. She notices that he is wearing a ring on his right hand, with the same cross-like symbol as Dominik's ring. Grace snaps back to the moment and states,

"I really couldn't see as well as the others. They had night-vision goggles."

The Prosecuting Counselor proceeds to lead Grace's testimony,

"So, the sergeant ordered his men on a berserk killing spree of the township at a sacred site and lied to you to cover it up!"

The Defense Counselor angrily stands up from behind the table,

"Your honor, I object and move to strike the Prosecuting Counselor's last statement on the grounds that he is leading the witness!"

"Objection granted. Prosecutor, I ask that you respect my courtroom." The Judge orders.

"I have no more questions for this witness, Your Honor," states the Prosecuting Counselor.

The Judge turns to Grace and tells her,

"You may step down."

The Prosecution calls Max, the pilot, to the stand.

"Take your time Sergeant Nazario, and describe for the court members on the panel what you saw." The Prosecuting Counselor states.

Max lifts her face from her palms and starts crying,

"The scene was the most awful thing I've witnessed in all my years of service."

She looks over at the Prosecuting Counselor,

"Body parts were strewn everywhere...a religious site was demolished."

Then, as another tear rolls down her cheek, she looks over at the panel.

"This man is a heartless maniac and doesn't deserve to wear that uniform."

The Defense Counselor abruptly stands up from behind the table,

"Your honor, I move to strike the witness's comment. That is her opinion and for the panel to decide."

The Judge responds,

"I agree. Motion granted."

The Defense and Prosecution deliver their closing arguments and places Eric's fate in the hands of the panel. The court members on the panel deliberate for about an hour and then return with their verdict.

The Judge proceeds to read the verdict and issue Eric's punishment.

"Sergeant Lansing, a panel of your peers has found you guilty of leading your men into reckless combat behavior, endangering the life of a US civilian, and killing many other non-combatants. You will be immediately, dishonorably discharged from the United States Marine Corps."

CHAPTER XIII

THE CONTRACT

After being railroaded and then discharged by the military for crimes he didn't commit, Eric decided to move back to his hometown and live with his father until he had sorted things out. He found himself sitting in his old room looking at pictures of his sister. Back in the one place I thought I would never see again, he thought to himself.

Eric walks downstairs and out to the mailbox every day in the hopes of receiving mail from his former squad members, asking him how things were going. He especially wanted to hear how their new squad leader wasn't as good a leader as he had been. But with each passing day, he began feeling depressed and discouraged at having to return to his hometown.

Finally, after about two months, Eric decided to glance through his dad's wooden liquor cabinet. He felt that drinking was the best way to forget how everything he loved had been taken away. He felt wounded, as though his core self had been removed. As more days passed and he emptied more bottles, his external attitude appeared to show how he felt about himself. For only the second time in his life, he felt out of control. He had stopped shaving, and his appearance was becoming shaggy and unkempt.

After the third month, Eric decided to walk to the park to feed the pigeons. Entering the park, he sees a squirrel darting from one of the trees. Then, Eric sees a blur suddenly dart on top of the squirrel enveloping it. Eric blinked and looked again. He noticed a hawk had grabbed the frantic creature and flew off into the sky. Poor little bastard, Eric thought to himself in the back of his mind. He felt so down that he wished he had been lucky enough to have his misery ended so swiftly.

Eric sees a green park bench and sits down. He reaches into a small paper bag and pulls out a hand full of crumbs. He carelessly tosses them on the ground in front of him. Immediately, pigeons and other small birds begin to fly towards the crumbs to enjoy the free lunch. He relishes this moment of solitude. It provides him a moment to let his mind wander about how things could have turned out.

It's another mild summer day, just like every other. It's not nearly as hot as it would get at the base after his morning run. Eric took a long deep breath as he gazed toward the sun - the king of the desert; he longed for the scorching heat of the desert. The desert sun offered the opportunity to fight for your right to live, where the fearless and most brilliant survived. The sun and desert challenged him to get up early and fight to be the best every day. That sun made him stronger. He knew it was the same sun, but somehow this meandering sun was without purpose. The Midwestern sun was no king in Eric's heart.

Eric closed his eyes momentarily. When he opened them he could hear the kids playing on the swings in the sand behind him. He thought about how strange this place was to him, as opposed to his surroundings back at the base.

To Eric's surprise, a limousine pulls up on the street directly down the path to his left. He begins to wonder who would be pompous enough to be driving a limo around this town. As the vehicle comes to a stop, the driver, dressed in an all-black suit, exits the vehicle. He walks around to the door facing Eric and opens it. Initially, the limousine door slightly blocked Eric's view of the passenger. Eric leans forward as he begins to wonder if the governor is in town or someone of similar importance.

The first thing Eric noticed was a pair of shiny black dress shoes touching the pavement. The passenger begins to stand up, and Eric can finally see who's making the grand entrance.

"F'n unbelievable," Eric says under his breath as he shakes his head in disbelief.

Holding a large manila envelope in his hand, Dominik steps out of the limo. He places the envelope under his arm as he tells the driver to wait; the driver nods, closes the door and stands next to it. Dominik begins casually walking toward the bench where Eric is feeding birds.

"Dominik, what are you doing here?" Eric asks, feeling irritated that Dominik had interrupted the pleasantry of his small-town vibe.

"I have a business proposition for you, Eric." Dominik steps closer.

"Go away Dominik." Eric blurts out.

"Coming to this little town you call home wasn't exactly my choice. Besides, you haven't found our company's stolen property. It's still out there and able to do a lot of harm. At least give me a few minutes to hear me out." Dominik states in a calm yet direct tone.

Eric glances at Dominik with a 'like I care' expression on his face before returning to carelessly tossing crumbs to the pigeons. Then, after a moment, he turns back to face Dominik.

"Where were you with all your highbrow money when I was being railroaded for war crimes? I could have used a proposition then." Eric fumes angrily.

"Sometimes things happen for reasons that are beyond comprehension," says Dominik, attempting to speak philosophically.

"Sorry, I would love to help, but my calendar is booked solid," Eric states sarcastically as he begins tossing larger portions of crumbs to hungry gatherers.

Dominik haphazardly points to the park pigeons scouring around the two men.

"Yes, I can see that."

Dominik looks down at the brown bag containing the pigeon crumbs. Then, touching it as little as possible, he attempts to move the bag towards Eric, making enough room for himself to sit down.

"Well, I told Grace you wouldn't listen, but she asked me to try. She's always been headstrong and obstinate." Dominik says reflectively in an unusually soft tone.

"We contracted with another military unit to retrieve the virus, but we lost contact with them. Grace was able to pinpoint their last general location. We need a real team to protect Grace while she infiltrates the terrorist's systems. If you decide to help us, we are willing to compensate you more than you could imagine. I know that you will be successful. Grace can finally locate the virus, and in the meantime, you can help bring some of our boys home. Besides, Grace refuses to work with anyone else but you."

Dominik begins to stand up; he looks woefully at Eric as he speaks.

"So, if you don't care about yourself, think about Grace. Think about the men that are captured and possibly hurt, then read the contents of that envelope."

Dominik tosses the large manila envelope he was carrying onto the bench next to Eric. The envelope lands with a slapping sound when it hits the bench. Dominik turns and strolls back to the limousine. After he sits comfortably inside, the driver closes the door and walks back around to the driver's side.

Eric had enough of Dominik's pompous behavior. He returned home and walked up the stairs back to his room. He tosses the envelope on his bed, finds a bottle of Crown Royal, lifts it to his lips, takes a drink, then lays across his bed and falls asleep.

When Eric awakens, feeling slightly sober, he sits up on the bed. He decides that it can't do any harm to look into the envelope's contents. He pulls out the contents and begins to read. It's probably a job offer from Dominik to be his new driver and lap dog, Eric thought to himself. To his surprise, it was an offer to form a joint security business with Dominik as a founding partner.

Eric thinks this is possibly good news and decides to share this with his dad. He walks through the house looking for his father. Eric's dad was in the backyard on his John Deere. Eric yelled to his father to come inside because there was something he wanted to discuss. After hearing about Dominik's business proposal, his dad decides it would be a good idea to have the contract reviewed by an attorney in town.

The next day Eric and his dad drive to the lawyer's office. They find the lawyer on the phone in his office when they arrive. The lawyer holds up his hand, asking for them to wait. The duo takes a seat in the waiting area. After waiting fifteen minutes, the Attorney calls them into his office to review the contract. He looks it over, and before he could speak, Eric asks,

"What do you think? Is there a clause to pay back the loan at 50% interest or something?" Eric asks with suspicion in his voice.

"Well, I'm no big city lawyer, but as far as I can tell, it all seems legitimate. This contract states that Eric would own 49% of the company. For 51% ownership, Global Unity would wholly fund the venture, providing Eric's executive salary for two years, and pay off the loan on your dad's house. In addition, it states here, he can select and hire the personnel for the security team," the lawyer adds. Eric's dad writes the lawyer a check, and then they leave the lawyer's office. They drive to the park to discuss the attorney's comments about the contract. They sit on the bench where Eric recently spoke to Dominik.

"Son, this may be the opportunity you are looking for." Eric's dad says. His voice was warm and encouraging.

Eric starts to doubt his sudden good fortune. "There's something about this, dad. That guy is a rich sleaze. Why would he help me? It's too easy."

Eric's dad placed his hand on Eric's shoulder and squeezed. Eric notices his hand looked a little frailer than he remembers as a kid.

"Son, look around. You have many questions, and the answers aren't going to be found here. You have talents that will be wasted here. This could be the opportunity you need to use them." His dad spoke with hope in his voice.

Eric felt reassured by his father's words. He's always there for me, providing me with ideas of hope and a better future, Eric thought to himself. At that moment, he felt as though a weight had been lifted from his shoulders.

CHAPTER XIV

H. H. PRIVATE SECURITY SERVICES

Thirty days after signing the contract to form a subsidiary security company, Eric's new company leases office space in downtown Seattle. Eric decided to stay at a hotel near the building. True to his old form, he woke before the sun rose and went for a morning run to get his mind sharp for the day. He felt good about himself again. After his run, he showered, walked to the closet and opened it. Hanging, there was a garment bag with a note attached, "Congratulations, Love Dad." Eric quickly unzipped the bag and proudly dressed in the dark blue suit. Eric wanted to arrive earlier than his new staff so he could greet everyone personally. As he left his hotel room, Eric felt like a man with a mission to conquer the world.

Upon arrival, Eric walks through the building's main reception area and glances at the directory. He briefly scanned down the list; a slight smile appeared when he found what he was looking for, *Hell Hounds Private Security Services* - ninth floor. He couldn't have been happier, and he knew his dad was proud of him as well. He had another opportunity for a new start, and he was going to make the most of it.

As Eric approached the elevator, he remembered his last conversation with Dominik earlier in the week. Dominik was surprisingly pleasant as he informed Eric that he wanted to be a good partner. He had taken the liberty of queuing up some prospective clients to get Eric started. Eric remembers thinking maybe Dominik wasn't such a pompous snob after all.

Eric pushed the button for the ninth floor and began strategizing his meeting with prospective clients. Good first impressions would be necessary for the company brand. Eric desired to build a reputation of reliability first. Shouldn't be too different from briefing the brass at the base, he pondered to himself.

Eric assumed Dominik's initial, prospective clients would be other rich pompous snobs who needed protection. Hopefully, his first contract was to babysit their rich kids as they partied in Ibiza. That way, he could have some fun too. Eric glanced up at the elevator's digital numbers as they counted up. ...07...08. Or, maybe the contract would be to ensure proprietary products arrived safely at their destination. As he thought more about it, he figured it's probably best not to take on a risky mission the first time out, but he was anxious to get started. He would also need to start interviewing security personnel immediately.

The elevator chimed softly as the digital number changed to 09, signaling he'd reached his destination floor. Exiting the elevator, he noticed a white motion-sensing security camera above his head. As he glanced up and down the hallway looking for his office suite, to his surprise, there was only one door on this floor. He slowly began to realize his office encompassed the entire ninth floor.

Walking up to the secure entrance, he takes a deep breath as he reads the name on the door, "Hell Hounds Private Security Services." Holy shit, how am I going to pay for all this? He thought to himself. Eric pulls a lanyard out from under his royal blue dress shirt then swipes his ID badge. The door makes a click sound as a tiny light on the badge reader turns from red to green.

Well, I've come this far; I may as well take the full tour, he thought. Eric closes his eyes, pushes open the door, and steps inside the room. Letting the door close behind him, he slowly opens his eyes and instinctively begins to focus his mind on memorizing every detail of the suite entrance.

Eric's smile quickly fades; to his surprise, the office wasn't as he had requested. Instead of having solid metal-style office furniture, the entire reception area was modern and filled with elaborate art. Nothing here suggested a reliable, sturdy, dependable security company. The only thing this office suggested was...Dominik. This had Dominik's signature all over it. He just couldn't leave things alone; he just had to have control.

What pompous S.O.B, Eric thought in anger. Eric felt this was Dominik's way of reminding him that it was his money. Just as Eric was considering calling Dominik to give him a piece of his mind, he heard a soft, distinctively feminine voice emanating directly across from him. Directly across from the entry was the reception area. Eric moved a few steps closer to look at the receptionist and hear what she was saying. The receptionist was seated behind the reception counter and wore a soft-phone headset. The headset had a blinking indigo light. She smoothly touched the blinking light and spoke with the most welcoming sounding voice Eric had ever heard.

"H H Private Security Services. How may I assist you?" She smiles as she glances in Eric's direction. She then stands up to greet Eric and motions for him to move closer as she continues her conversation... "Yes, he is in a meeting. May I take a message?" the receptionist spoke into the soft-phone.

As she stood to greet Eric, he took note that she was tall and slender. Her outfit was just as professional as her speech. She wore a long-sleeve black mock turtleneck with a small white pearl choker. She also wore a fitted hounds-tooth pencil skirt. He could tell from the way she stood that she was poised with a toned physical build. He reasoned that in order to be so toned, she must have an extremely rigid workout routine, or maybe she's a part-time athlete, Eric thought to himself.

"Yes, understood. Have a wonderful day," she said, speaking softly into the headset once again.

Her blonde hair was so light it was practically white. Her hair was pulled back into a perfectly tight bun, and not a single hair was out of place. She held her bun in place for a slight flair with two ornate chopsticks with familiar-looking symbols on the top.

"Good morning, Mr. Lansing. Dominik said you would be arriving early," she said in a low tone. "Would you like an espresso brought to your office?" she asked and gestures toward a shiny new black and chrome system.

It had several chrome buttons, levers, and a digital display. Eric assumed that the receptionist achieved some sort of technical certification to make espressos with that gizmo.

"No, thank you...What's your name?" Eric asked, controlling his emotions.

He didn't want to misdirect his frustration with Dominik towards the new administrator. She smiled a pearly white grin that lit up the room, then slowly placed her hands together on the desk, relaxing her shoulders as she leaned forward over the desk.

"Courtney, sir...Mr. Lansing. May I say what an honor it is to be working here. Dominik has told the entire staff about how you kept Grace safe under fire. You're practically a hero."

Eric could only wonder what sort of tall tales Dominik had told these people. Moreover, he wondered if he also mentioned to them about his dishonorable discharge.

"Well, um, thank you, Courtney." Trying to ignore her apparent flirtatious overtone. He thought it best not to get in trouble with his staff on the first day.

"I heard your phone conversation, and you said someone is in a meeting? Eric asked.

Courtney straightens up and regains her professional composure...

"Oh yes, Dominik. He is currently in a meeting in the conference room."

Eric wondered why Dominik would arrange a meeting this early without him. I thought we were going to be partners in this. Eric could feel himself becoming upset with Dominik all over again.

"He's with your new security team. They are waiting for you." the receptionist stated.

"The new security team?" Eric repeated, becoming agitated.

Am I not even going to get the chance to hire my own security team? Dominik has gone too far now! I will have to tell the new team, thank you for your interest, but everyone will need to interview with me. Eric thought as he became more agitated. Eric abruptly turns to the left and begins to walk away. Suddenly he stops and looks at Courtney, realizing he doesn't know where the conference room is located. Sensing Eric's impatience, Courtney points to the right; Eric changes direction and begins his walk to confront Dominik.

"Continental breakfast will be served shortly," Courtney shouts as Eric marches off toward the conference room.

Eric finds Dominik standing near the conference room entrance, reviewing documents with a few personnel nodding in agreement. Eric could only assume these were more of *Hell Hound's Security* personnel hired by Dominik without including him.

"Dominik, I would like to have a word with you about what's going on here," Eric states, forcefully interrupting their conversation. "What is this furniture? Courtney over there says you already hired a security team?" Eric's tone was as if he were speaking to first-day cadets.

Dominik calmly dismisses the personnel gathered around him.

"The contract states you can pick the security personnel, and we can choose everything else."

Dominik states as he turns toward the conference room door. He swipes his badge and begins punching in a code. He slowly opens the door to the conference room. As the door swings open, Eric turns to look into the conference room.

"I may have slightly overstepped when I took the liberty of offering jobs to your former military squad." Dominik utters to Eric.

After the door swung open completely, Eric could see the faces of those seated around the table: Darryl, Cesar, Sam, and of course, Grace. Seated next to Grace was a blonde guy who didn't look familiar, but at the moment, Eric didn't care. Darryl, who was seated nearest to the door, stood and saluted Eric. The other squad members then stood and saluted Eric in turn. Eric was overcome with happiness to see these misfits. He couldn't contain himself. He bolted into the conference room and over to Darryl; he practically picked him up off the floor when he hugged him, which wasn't an easy feat.

"What the hell are you guys doing here?" Eric asked happily as he went around the table, warmly embracing his former team members.

"After your trial, Dominik negotiated with the government for an honorable discharge, then offered us employment at a new security firm," Darryl explained.

After greeting his former squad, Eric turned to Grace. Grace slowly walked over to Eric and hugged him. She wore a triumphant smile as she opened her arms for a hug. Dominik pulled out a chair and offered Eric a seat at the table. Eric, satisfied that he was finally among friends, relaxed, and took the seat offered by Dominik at the head of the table. I've experienced some terrible missions with these soldiers, and lived to get drunk and party with these guys. They were like brothers, Eric thought to himself as he looked around the table.

CHAPTER XV

UNWANTED MISSION PERSONNEL

"Eric, with your permission, is it okay to begin?" Dominik asks.

Eric nods his head in agreement. Dominik picks up the small remote from the edge of the table near Eric.

"Now on to why everyone is here." Dominik clicks the power button on the remote.

In the moments before Dominik begins his presentation, Eric takes an opportunity to scan the conference room. As his eyes darted around the room, he realized the frank sterility of the room. The walls were white, the chairs were white, and the cabinets were also sterile white. The only thing that wasn't white was the large rectangular glass meeting table everyone sat around. The glass table was clear except for the white light beaming through the perimeter of the table. The large table could seat about 15-20 people. The room had all the charm of a hospital operating room.

"I hope everyone will be equally satisfied with the maiden mission as they are with the team. This will be the only mission I organize. As stated in our contract, Eric will be in charge from now on." Dominik continued.

Once Dominik presses the power button, a large pane of clear glass rises from the white cabinet against the wall. As the glass completes its ascent, it displays a three-dimensional company logo, *Global Unity Electronics Corporation*™.

"Man, Global Unity Electronics Corporation owns practically every-thing," Sam utters.

Ignoring Sam's comments, Eric continues his scan of the room; he finds that in stark contrast to the bright white walls were pictures of planets. Behind the rising pane of glass hung a foreboding flat, black, thinly framed picture of a ringed planet. From his distance, and with the light dimming, he could barely make out the embossed lettering underneath the framed picture. It looked like an h, with a cross on top of it.

♄

Eric began wondering if the rich compete against each other by putting their eccentric behavior on display?

A high-resolution aerial satellite photo of a Middle Eastern town appears on the screen.

"Terrorists using our biochemical asset wiped out the entire population of the town," Dominik remarks as he continues his presentation.

Images of dismembered bodies huddled together with ripped flesh quickly cycle through the monitor. Some images show the town's people with traces of a thick black substance on their bodies and others with the same black substance dripping from their mouths.

"Naturally, we would have sent the military to complete this mission, but the Hell Hounds squad was *indisposed* during this time. So, our Directors decided to hire a private military team to track and terminate the terrorist.

The image on the screen changes to a picture of four men smiling, standing close together dressed in combat gear.

"The team tracked the terrorist down to this abandoned ancient Pagan temple."

The image on the screen brightens then changes again to display an old temple cut from a large desert stone.

"This was the last we heard from them. Fortunately, one of our ground scanning satellites was nearing the area; this type of tech is often used to peer under the trees in South America when looking for ruins. A deep infrared scan of the temple revealed something interesting."

The image on the monitor changes again, displaying a birds-eye view inside the temple. It then zooms underneath the temple to display the outline of long passages and multiple large rooms.

"The satellite revealed massive passageways, rooms, and halls underneath the temple. It appears this temple may have been built on the ruins of an ancient underground city. We scanned as much as possible before the satellite was out of range. This team's assignment will be to find and rescue the last mercenary team, and if possible, retrieve any corporate bio assets that may be present."

The conference room lights begin to brighten slowly, and Eric notices a black cube mounted to a stand in the center of the table. It caught his attention because it appeared remarkably smooth. It was divided into eight equal parts, similar to a Rubik's cube but all black. There were small symbols cut into each square. As far as Eric could tell, some of the symbols looked identical to those under the paintings on the walls and on Dominik's ring. He was tempted to examine it closer but thought better of the idea. Knowing Dominik, it was probably expensive and worth his entire executive salary, Eric thought. Dominik notices Eric inquisitively looking at the black cube in the center of the table.

"Ah, Eric, I see you have an eye for the unusual. This is, shall we say, a unique piece. This cube is made of a rare mineral; myth states it comes from the underworld and has transformative properties in its liquid state," Dominik proudly exclaims.

Yep, that proves my theory; wealthy eccentrics love to brag on their outlandish possessions, Eric continued thinking to himself.

Anticipating the end of Dominik's presentation, Eric begins to stand as he speaks to everyone at the table.

"Thank you, Dominik. I would like to begin our preparations for the mission."

As Dominik begins to respond, one of his assistants steps into the conference room and whispers into Dominik's ear.

"Ah, Eric, I'm not quite finished. I would be remiss if I failed to introduce a last-minute addition to your security team."

As Dominik nods, the assistant walks back to the conference room door and opens it wide. As the door opened and the figure stepped through, it shocked Eric. Even in her uniform, you could tell she had the toned body of professional athletes. Her hair was pulled back into a tight bun exposing her sun-kissed complexion. He composed himself after realizing he was probably showing disdain for the person who had just entered the room.

"Is it that snitch!" whispered Cesar.

"Ah, hell naw, I don't believe this!" said Darryl under his breath.

"I would like to introduce you to the "Hell Hounds" and their team leader Eric. They will be in charge of security. Max, please be seated." Dominik offered her a chair.

Max, feeling the intensity of the room, waved off Dominik's offer of the chair.

"Thank you, but I prefer to stand," Max said assertively.

She wasn't sure how this meeting would go but felt it best to be prepared for anything. Max knew before she walked into the room she would need to gain Eric's trust before the mission and, by extension, the trust of his team.

"We know who she is, and we don't want a traitor on our team," Eric spoke through gritted teeth. "Dominik, we agree to everything except adding Max. This appears to be a simple job." Eric adds.

Max remained perfectly still and took a moment to glance at Eric's team without turning her head. Then, turning to face Eric, looks him directly in the eyes and begins to speak loud enough to ensure everyone could hear, without changing her facial expression.

"With respect to Eric and his...*hounds,* you don't usually call me in for *simple* missions. So, I'm assuming Eric and his team don't know what they may encounter out there, and they'll probably be in over their heads. You were smart to add me to the security detail," Max stated bluntly.

Eric was becoming angrier at Max's audacity to say they couldn't handle a search and rescue mission. He was about to reply to Max when Dominik held up his hand to stop the banter.

"Eric, in the contract, it states that Global Unity can assign contractors to go along with the security team if their presence may be beneficial to corporate interest. So Max, for example, is one such contractor. Let's consider her, the corporation's insurance policy. You may find her helpful on the mission."

At this point, Eric was fuming. Bastard, he did it to me again. I am not sure how he always manages to one-up me, he thought to himself.

With the addition of Max to the team by Dominik, the tension in the air had become thick enough to cut with a butter knife, and the meeting abruptly came to an end. As the team started to pack up, Eric began casually speaking with Grace, attempting to catch up on lost time. Max takes a deep breath, walks over to Eric, and

clears her throat to get his attention. Eric turns to face her with
a look of disdain.

"Eric, I want you to trust me. Please, give me an hour to con-
vince you I can be an asset. If not, I'll tell Dominik myself that
I'm dropping out. I'm only asking for an opportunity," Max said,
letting her voice trail off to express vulnerability.

As Darryl begins to collect his notes, he notices Max pleading
with Eric. He knows Eric is a sucker for bleeding hearts, so he
decides he'd better run some interference. He approaches Eric and
Max before he exits the conference room.

"The guys are getting together after this to celebrate our
reunion. You coming, Eric?" Darryl asks.

Eric looks at Darryl then looks at Max. Max was doing her
best to appear sincere.

"Nah, you guys go ahead. Have a few drinks on me." Eric says
to Darryl.

Darryl hopes Eric realizes that he can't trust her.

"Alright, well, that's going to get expensive," he says.

Darryl begins to exit the conference room as he walks around
Eric; He makes eye contact with Max when he gets behind Eric.
Then, he uses three fingers to form a gun and aims it in Max's
direction. He turns and walks away. Ignoring Darryl's threats, Max
turns her attention back to Eric.

"I'll take that as a sign you'll at least hear me out. Meet me at
the Air Force base at 0500... I have something I want to share with
you," she stated in a grateful tone.

CHAPTER XVI

THE FLIGHT

Eric arrives at the Air Force base, checks in, receives his guest pass, and directions to the meet-up location. He finds the appropriate building and entrance.

"Do you know where I can find Max? She's a pilot here." Eric asks a Private.

"Yes, sir, she's waiting for you out on the tarmac. She left these for you." The private hand's Eric some clothing and boots. "You can change over there. The tarmac is down this way, sir," stated the Private.

Eric exits the locker room wearing a flight suit and steel-toe boots. Following the private's directions, he makes his way onto the tarmac. He sees Max wearing an identical flight suit and shades. As he walks over to her location, he notes all the different jets, F13, Warthog, C10.

Once Eric reaches Max, she says to him,

"Wasn't sure you were going to meet me."

"I wasn't sure either. What is it that you want to say?" Eric snaps impatiently.

"Thank you for giving me a chance....I figured we could do some trust-building flying exercises."

She starts walking. Eric follows her, and they stop near an old, small jet that appears to be barely usable.

"Well, let's get it started," Max says.

Eric, feeling let down, responds,

"Does that thing even fly?"

Max, surprised at his comment, points in the direction of another jet.

"Not that one, the one next to it." Max quips.

Eric looks past the shabby jet.

"I'm not familiar with this one," Eric says.

"It's an AV-8B II trainer," Max says smiling.

"Trainer?" Eric says inquisitively.

Max's smile widens.

"Have you ever flown a V.T.O.L.?" Max asks.

"They don't let *Jarheads* like me fly jets," Eric states.

"Well, you're free from those limits now. Climb aboard, Sergeant." Max tells him.

Max climbs the small ladder behind Eric and instructs him how to buckle himself into the copilot's seat and how to securely wear the helmet. She then gives brief descriptions of how to read the dizzying array of instruments. Eric nods in acknowledgment, but he barely understands most of it.

Max descends from the trainee's cockpit and climbs into the trainer's cockpit. She straps herself in, puts on her helmet, and tests the communication between herself and Eric.

"Hey, let's make a wager. If you vomit, you buy me a beer. If you pass out, you buy me two beers, and I get to tell the whole story to the rest of the Hounds."

"What if I'm better than you think? What do I win?" Eric quips.

"Oh, I seriously doubt that, but I'm sure you'll think of something," Max said slyly.

The tarmac officer signals to Max the engine is ready, and

the tower notifies her as to which runway to take. Max salutes to the officer and starts maneuvering the AV-8B II following the appropriate colored line to the approved runway. The ride down the tarmac bounced Eric uncomfortably up and down in his seat. For some reason, he thought the drive would be smoother. When they arrive at the runway, Max says over the comms to Eric,

"Hold on to your cherry. This should be fun."

Suddenly, Eric experiences the most confusing sensation. Instead of being thrust back into his seat as with the normal jet takeoff, his stomach was pushed down toward the seat as the jet lifted straight up into the air. He had forgotten that this jet was a Vertical Take-off and Landing type of aircraft. The V.T.O.L. slowly glided a few yards before Max pointed the nose skyward and then accelerated.

As soon as Eric adjusted himself to be pushed down in the seat, the AV-8B II lurched forward and shoved him back into his seat. They were headed straight for the clouds. Eric was thrilled.

"I want you to trust me, but I also need to know I can trust you when you are out of your comfort zone," Max shares with Eric.

An F-18 comes up on the side, and Eric can see the pilot salute Max before he trails off.

"We're clear. Take the stick," Max instructs Eric.

"Now?" Eric exclaimed, surprised.

"No, after we crash into the side of a mountain," Max exclaims sarcastically.

Eric places a tight grip on the throttle as Max talks him through reading the instruments. Max notices the rush of excitement overcoming Eric.

"How are you doing?" Max smiles as she asks.

"Whooo, F-an A-mazing!" Eric shouts excitedly into the headset.

Clouds zoom by; it was the most exhilarating thing Eric ever experienced. He never felt freer in his life. He loved the experience and didn't want it to end.

About an hour later, the Harrier slowly descends from the sky, and Max effortlessly maneuvers the plane down on the runway. She maneuvers the plane back to the tarmac and kills the engine. She signals for the privates to bring over ladders so that she and Eric can exit the plane. As they climb down the ladder, Max begins to speak to Eric.

"You did alright up there, Sarge. I really thought you would blow chunks," Max said lightheartedly.

Eric and Max begin their walk back to the door that leads inside the building to change out of their flight suits. Before Eric enters the door, Max steps in front of him and turns to face him. Standing in front of him, she now blocked his entrance to the door. Surprised, Eric looked at her to see if he could figure out what was going on.

She lightly puts her hand on Eric's chest to halt his movement and then says to him,

"Sarge, let me pay off my "L" by buying you a beer at a bar near here. We can go in my car. It'll only take a few minutes to get there."

Just as Eric was about to speak, Max quickly spun around and then walked into the building. Apparently, she's not taking no for an answer, Eric thought as he watched her confidently stride down the hallway.

Eric finishes putting on his jeans, shirt, and hat in the changing room. He wasn't sure of what had just happened. So now we're getting drinks? He thought. He exits the changing room and walks down the winding hallways. As he walks past the guard manning the front desk, he pushes open the front door, where he sees Max in the parking lot sitting on the hood of her car. As Eric got closer, he noticed Max's car was a real beauty.

He walks around the car, lightly touching the paint. Max walks in the opposite direction to the driver's side door, opens it, and motions for Eric to get in. Eric still felt the adrenaline in his body after his triumphant flight, and he wasn't about to miss a chance to drive this car.

He eagerly hops in the car and grips the steering wheel. Eric thought, we'll have a few drinks; I'll politely thank Max for the flight, then let her know there's no way she's going to join my team. She'll probably throw her drink in my face, but it'll be worth it to see her pissed, Eric thought to himself.

Max hurries around to the passenger door, opens it, and slowly slides into the passenger seat. At this moment, Eric noticed that she was still wearing her flight suit.

"Don't you want to change?" Eric asked curiously.

"Nah, let's grab some beers first. I'll change into something more comfortable later." Max states nonchalantly.

She hands Eric the keys, and he starts the car. The engine starts with an easy mellow hum. Eric backs out of the parking space, and drives off the lot towards the gates to exit the base grounds.

CHAPTER XVII

THE SONG

When they pulled into the parking lot of the bar, it was mostly empty.

"How do you like my ride?" Max leaned in closer to Eric and smiled as she spoke.

Eric glances at Max's smile and pauses before he speaks.

"Not sure which ride you're speaking of," Eric says, attempting to avoid answering the question.

Max doesn't hesitate to push further and states in a sly, low voice,

"Which ride do you want to talk about?"

"The training or this car? They're both a smooth, fast ride," Eric states and smiles back.

Eric parks the car, turns off the engine, and hands the keys to Max. She playfully takes the keys, exits the car, and walks to the rear of the car. She lifts the trunk door blocking Eric's view. She retrieves her duffle bag and then lowers and closes the trunk. As she throws the duffle bag over her shoulder, Eric politely asks,

"Don't you want to leave your bag in the car?"

Max stated pointedly,

"No sir, I have all my essentials in here. I believe in always being prepared."

Eric begins to wonder what is in the bag that could be so important. Seems as though she would be more worried about someone stealing the car than some old bag, he thought to himself.

Together, the duo begins to walk toward the door; Eric leans in ahead of Max and opens the door as he motions for her to enter. As they walk into the bar, Eric realizes the place is more upscale than the outside led him to believe. Approaching the bar counter, he notices the place has a small stage and an open area, presumably to gather and watch a band. Eric wonders if there'll be a country band playing later. He hopes Max doesn't press him too early about joining him. I'd like to at least hear the band before the beer gets tossed into my face.

As Eric and Max approach the bar, the bartender turns, spots Max, and smiles in her direction. He then puts both his hands on his hips as he speaks in Spanish and English. His voice was a lot higher than Eric suspected.

"Max, qué pasa chica, what can I get you?"

Max smiles, acknowledging the bartender, and nods her head in Eric's direction.

"Papa Jac for me and whatever he wants."

The bartender finishes putting away some glasses then walks over to Eric and Max as they take their seats at the bar. The bartender leans towards Max and places his hands on the bar. He looks Eric up and down as if he were studying a prize bull. He lowers his left shoulder, pouts his lips, and points to Eric.

"...and how about for you señor mucho caliente?"

The bartender leans in slightly closer to Max and feigns whispering.

"This is the sexiest date you've had in some time, Max."

Eric responds immediately by waving his hands in front of his chest as if to call off a foul football play.

"Date? It's not like that man...er girl."

Eric wasn't quite sure how to address the bartender. He figured it best to cover all bases.

"I'm only here for the free beer."

As the bartender straightens up, he puckers his lips, cocks his head to the side, looks back and forth from Eric to Max.

"Is that so? If she's not your type, then maybe I am. I get off around midnight."

Max and the bartender both start giggling at his brazen, flirtatious attempts. Finally, Eric, not sure how to respond to the comments, or the giggles, blurts out,

"Hey, you serve, um, Yuengling?"

Eric figured that drink would take some time for the bartender to locate. However, the bartender, looking impressed, responds,

"Ah, a classic beer drinking man. Just my type."

The bartender winks at Eric, daintily turns and sashays away to gather their drinks. Max picks up the duffle bag she brought with her and places it on the bar counter. The bartender returns and sets their drinks down in front of them before hurrying off to serve the rush of customers entering the bar. Max takes a sip of her drink and begins to soften her voice as she begins to speak.

"I want to apologize to you, Eric. I never meant for things to happen this way, you know."

Eric, irritated, put the can of beer to his lips, tilted his head back, and gulped. The mere mention of the trial right on the onset was ruining the taste of his classic beer.

"I can't believe the panel fell for those crocodile tears. You were giving an Oscar performance up there," Eric stated sternly without raising his voice.

He didn't want to make a scene. However, some commotion from the stage area allowed him to avoid the subject of the conversation. He turns around slightly, noticing the band had begun setting up on stage.

Finally, maybe I can pretend to listen to her. The band doesn't even have to be all that good as long as it drowns out her rambling, he thought to himself. After a few moments, the band was ready, and the lights dropped as the musicians started to play. Eric became even more annoyed as he realized the band wasn't playing country music at all. Instead, the band was playing Latin music.

Nothing was going in Eric's favor this evening. In the heat of the moment, Eric decides to confront Max and tell her everything he was holding inside since he saw her on the witness stand. Eric turns to look Max in the face to give her a piece of his mind.

"You know good and well we didn't slaughter civil..."

Max stood up and began to slowly unzip her flight jumpsuit at the bar. He forgot his thought as he noticed she was gazing into his eyes.

"Let me try to make it up to you," Max states in a seductive tone.

Her drab flight suit suddenly fell to the floor around her black military boots, revealing a cherry red, figure-hugging, low cut halter dress with tiny straps over the shoulders. The dress had elegant ruffles along the side that revealed her shapely toned legs. Eric noticed the slit went dangerously close up her right hip.

"I only want a chance to show you what I can do," Max continued.

She reaches into the bag and pulls out lipstick. She carefully applied lipstick, which was as cherry red as her dress. After applying her lipstick, she smiles, puts her hands on her hips and starts to sway to the beat of the Latin rhythms of the band. She steps out of the flight suit that was now on the floor, sits back at the bar, and slowly crosses her legs one at a time to remove her steel-toe boots. Next, she pulls a pin out of her tight bun and shakes her hair free. Finally, she reaches in her bag once again and pulls out a pair of red thinly strapped shoes. She places them on the floor and daintily steps into them. She quickly snatches her flight suit from the floor and tosses it in the bag.

"Well, how do I look?" She asks Eric.

Eric was amazed. Before he could utter a word, Max quickly takes another sip of her drink, then grabs Eric's hand, leads him to the dance floor, stating,

"Mi canción favorita! Por favor, come salsa with me!"

Eric looked around, and suddenly the dance floor was filled with couples dancing. Men were effortlessly twirling their partners. Eric, who had seen many battles in the field, suddenly had an emotional response that he didn't experience much...embarrassment.

"Um, I don't know how to salsa."

Even though Eric was resistant, Max dragged him closer to the stage. When Max found a spot for them to dance, she smiled broadly, putting her finger to her lips. She stood on her toes, then pulled herself close to Eric's ear so he could hear her over the music.

"Shh...Close your eyes. Become one with the music."

Eric closed his eyes. Max grabbed his hands and placed them on her hips as she swayed them side to side. Max placed her arms over his shoulders and gently encouraged him to step forward and then back in rhythm with her moves. As he felt the movement of her hips swaying to the music, Eric focused on the beat of the music. As he held his hands on Max's hips, he found himself drifting away.

But after only a few moments of dancing, Eric became self-conscious. I better check around to see if anyone was wondering how this *no rhythm gringo* scored a dance with such a fabulous dancer. He briefly opened his eyes and was surprised that no one was looking at him at all. Everyone was dancing to the sounds of the band. Eric loved the sounds of the horns playing. He had never had a dancing experience like this. It was exhilarating, although he hadn't danced much before at all.

Just as he felt he was getting the hang of the dance, he became distracted when the music lowered. This was the best he had felt in quite some time. Is the song over already? He thought to himself.

"Max, aqui...aqui!"

The band leader began to wave Max over to the stage. Everyone stopped dancing and began looking at Max and Eric, chanting,

"Max, Max, Max!"

Although the music is a bit lower. Max again gets on her toes and leans into Eric's ear to speak over the music,

"Don't go anywhere. I'll be right back."

Max steps onto the stage. The lead singer offers Max the mic stand. Max closes her eyes and pauses as she approaches the microphone. The band begins to play softly; Eric stares at her in anticipation. Softly at first, then all at once, a beautiful deep, rich voice sprung from her lips.

Esto no es fácil

Para que yo admita

Tengo un fuego adentro y algunas palabras que sé que no puedo mantener

Veo el amor convertirse en un espectáculo

Ya no es satisfactorio

¿No es cierto que el velo se desgarrado?

She delicately folds her arms across her chest and looks directly at Eric in a sweeping uncrossing motion as she sings. The music begins to crescendo...

No necesito nada perfecto, junta palabras bonitas

Quiero su verdadero amor

Algo que anhelo profundamente dentro de mis huesos

Max finishes her song, turns, looks at the band, holds up her hand, and then makes a fist. On cue, the music stops. Max belts out, "Uno...Dos...Tres!"

She drops her hand, and the band starts playing a high-energy song of complex percussion, piano, and bold trumpets. The crowd goes wild with applause, whistling and cheering at her performance.

Eric was awe-struck. Her voice was as strong and as beautiful as she was. What couldn't she do? He thinks his mouth may have been slightly opened during her performance. But he wasn't sure; he just hoped she didn't notice. Although he couldn't understand the words, he felt that it was a Spanish love song, or at least he hoped it was.

Max hops down off the stage and skips triumphantly towards Eric. She grabs his hands, placing her palm in his. She lifts their hands in the air as she dances them triumphantly around in a circle. Then, letting his left-hand fall, she slightly let go of the right, keeping their fingertips touching lightly. With his hands as her balance, she began to twirl in place in front of Eric. As the light reflected off her hair, blonde streaks flashed like rays of sunlight in Eric's mind as they went by.

Eric thought she would be dizzy from spinning, but he remembered she was a pilot. Spinning was probably second nature to her. Max completes her last turn, stops facing Eric, leans in close to him, puts her hand on his chest near his heart, and whispers,

"Let's leave here, Papi."

This time a slight tingle went up to his spine as he could feel her lips gently brushing against his ear. She gently squeezed Eric's hand and led him back to the bar counter. She grabs her bag and boots, and hands the boots to Eric to carry. Before Eric knew what was happening, they were heading out the front door.

The Bartender, after watching the couple leave, snaps his finger in a half-circle and says to himself,

"Now that was a date!"

CHAPTER XVIII

HELL HOUNDS REUNION

The Hell Hound's team meets at the Air Force Base at 4 a.m. to load their equipment onto the plane. The mood is light as the old team is happy to be working together on a mission again. The guys are laughing, telling jokes about former lovers and jokes about the missions that almost got them killed. Then, Darryl begins to change the discussion with one of his outlandish conspiracy theories.

"C'mon Sam, you and everyone else knows that the President is just a figurehead for the ancient shape-shifting serpent aliens from Orion's belt. They've been pulling the strings for ages."

Sam, caught off guard, isn't quite sure if Darryl is joking or not, and remarks,

"Ah man, I thought I heard some good ones from you, but this takes the cake."

Darryl rebuffs Sam's comments.

"Don't tell me you guys don't know about this? Seriously, everyone knows this one."

"So what you're saying, all these wars we fight and global poverty is just to satisfy some serpent people," Cesar asked.

"They manipulate world events to keep our third eye blind. Y'all feeling me?"

The team can hear the light footsteps of boots approaching. A small figure begins to approach the team from the shadows, interrupting the team's fun. Max shows up in her flight suit, boots, and a full flight bag hanging from her shoulder, then asks,

"Eric, where should I put my gear?"

Darryl says under his breath,

"Speaking of snakes."

Max feigned a smile as if she had just noticed Darryl.

"Hello...*Darryl*."

Sam and Cesar begin to grumble. They spot Grace and decide to help her with her equipment.

Eric felt uplifted after Max showed up. He politely points out the direction of a pile of equipment.

"Equipment to be loaded on the plane goes over there."

Max gives Eric a flirty smile and a wink right before she walks away, saying to him,

"Thanks!"

Darryl suddenly feels agitated as the joy of performing another mission with the boys fades.

"What the hell was that?"

Eric catches himself grinning in Max's direction.

"You heard Dominik. She's one of our pilots?" Eric quickly responds in an attempt to cover his emotions.

The thought of what may have transpired between Eric and Max agitates Darryl.

"Shit, you *slept* with her!"

Eric starts feigning ignorance.

"C'mon...I mean, what makes you think that?"

Darryl looks at him disappointed,

"Damn, come on, Eric! The lady gets you kicked out of the Corps, and you do the horizontal mambo with her!"

Eric chuckles out loud before he speaks.

"Well, it was more like a vertical Salsa."

Darryl's eyes began to bulge in their sockets.

"She's a *honey pot*, and you know it's bad luck to sleep with your teammates before, during, or *after* a mission."

Eric turns to Darryl and tries to look sincere.

"I didn't sleep with her. We went dancing."

Darryl snarls back,

"Look, whatever Eric. Just don't get the rest of us killed because you wanted to do the Lambada with a snitch."

Disgusted, Darryl pours out what's left of his water on the ground, tosses his bottle into the nearest recycle bin, and gets up, walking away to join Sam and Cesar.

CHAPTER XIX

STRANGE TURBULENCE

With a Hummer and all the other equipment loaded on the cargo plane, Max sits down in the cockpit with the main pilot. She places her headset on and begins running through their take-off procedures. In the transport section, the team begins to buckle themselves in for the long flight.

After a few hours of in-flight boredom, Grace, feeling out of sorts from being separated from her electronic devices, decides to walk over to the storage area to find her laptop bag. Max finishes her descent down the ladder from the cockpit and starts walking towards her seat in the transport area. While Grace walks to pick up her bag, Max keeps a watchful eye on her. Grace stumbles awkwardly during an air pocket. When Max arrives at her seat, she begins to strap herself in. Grace finds her bag, unzips it, verifies the laptop is in there, throws the opened laptop bag over her shoulder, then turns to navigate the turbulence back to her seat.

As Grace approaches where Max is seated, another bout of rough air turbulence begins. Max sees Grace approaching and begins to lean back in her chair; she shifts her left foot slightly forward as Grace attempts to pass. The tip of Max's boot was all that was needed to make Grace lose her footing. The combination of the turbulence and her misstep was enough to force Grace to take a step then begin to tumble backward, helplessly toward the hard metal floor of the plane. Several objects fall out of her unzipped bag.

Grace's perception of time changed; the entire moment occurred to her in slow motion. As she fell, her view rotated to the plane's ceiling as she tumbled backward. As if in the far distance, the slight pinging sounds of her encrypted USB sticks and USB card reader hitting the deck of the plane reached her ears. Grace closed her eyes tightly and instinctively constricted her muscles as she anticipated the back of her head hitting the same metal deck. She expected that the next sound reaching her ears would be from inside her head when her skull met the metal floor.

In anticipation of Grace's fall, Max slouches slightly in her chair, then positions her thighs and her left arm to interrupt Grace's backward descent. Instead of hitting the hard metal floor, Grace fell onto Max's toned lap. Max grabbed Grace's shoulder firmly, cradling Grace and preventing her from moving.

Surprised that she didn't hit the deck, Grace slowly opens her eyes to take note of what transpired. As she opens her eyes, she sees Max intently smiling and her face slowly moving in closer to hers. Grace had never been this close to Max before, and didn't quite know what to think. Max's face was now close enough to hers that she noticed how Max's eyes weren't only brown, but there was a hint of green, an almost hazel color. Grace felt as though she momentarily pierced Max's cold veil as she peered into her eyes. She could sense kindness and passion, but there was something else in her that was carefully hidden, but Grace could somehow sense it.

Max moved her left hand to seemingly embrace Grace. Her hand continued its gentle exploration across and down Grace's right hip. Max's hand then found its way into Grace's unzipped backpack. She loosens her grip as she lets something fall.

With Max smiling at her so intently and being held so firmly by Max, Grace felt the warmth of her toned body against her. She began to feel a little flush and embarrassed. She quickly stood up as the turbulence abated. When she realized she had found her equilibrium, she tried to make light of the situation.

"Apologies. I forgot my sea legs," Grace says, embarrassed.

Grace felt uncomfortable that their eye contact seemed to last moments too long.

"It's nothing." Max states, then pauses and asks suggestively, "Is this your first time?"

Grace's eyes widened as the question caught her by surprise.

"Excuse me?"

"You know, on a cargo plane?" Max muses.

As she straightened her tousled red hair, Grace began to relax with Max's clarifying question, but avoided answering and direct eye contact with her. Max continued speaking.

"Military jets often have a bumpy ride and lots of unnecessary turbulence; commercial jets are sleek and offer a smoother ride. As a *versatile* pilot, I take the opportunity to fly both types of jets. But regardless of the type, I'm always in control, and I bring all planes in for a smooth landing."

Max speaks confidently as she makes an airplane landing gesture with her hand. She then leans back in her seat, crosses her right leg over her left, puts her hands behind her head, closes her eyes, and begins to sleep.

Starting to feel slightly flustered by Max's comments, Grace averts her eyes away from Max. She then turns and hurries back to her seat. Finding her seat, she straps herself in. She takes a quick glance back at Max, who was still sitting in her seat, falling asleep as though nothing had happened.

This was the most contact Grace had with Max, and in truth,

she wasn't exactly sure how she should perceive Max's last comment. However, Grace did realize one thing from their encounter. The thing hidden in Max's eyes was pain. Grace knew that Max would do whatever it took to survive.

Across from Grace on the other side of the plane, Darryl pretended to be asleep and had observed the entire encounter. Well, that was weird. I wonder if Eric knows his girl doesn't mind having multiple lambada partners. A young redhead and a hot-headed Latina seems like it quickly becomes a wild party. Maybe you're a lucky S.O.B. after all. Darryl thinks to himself before he decides to get some sleep for the remainder of the trip.

An hour later, the pilot pushes the button that signals to the team that they've reached their destination. The team unhooks their straps and begins to put on their parachutes and check their equipment. Darryl moves into position to press the switches for the cargo door to open. He looks around to verify that everyone has begun their equipment check. When he presses the button, the door lowers into position, and a rush of biting cold air enters the transport bay. Finally, Darryl unhooks the Hummer and begins pushing it out of the back of the plane.

Max slants her eyes as she watches Eric assist Grace with her equipment. As he dotes over Grace, Max begins to wonder if Grace really needs help or was this all just an act. Max decides she'll keep watching, for now; she then stands up after checking her equipment for safety measures, and then runs toward the opening cargo door of the plane. She reaches the end, turns to the team, and yells over the gust of wind entering the plane.

"Last one to the ground is a pequeña coño," Max shouts before she places her helmet over her head.

She gives the team the one-finger salute and then effortlessly somersaults off the end of the lowered cargo door into the open air. As she exits her spin, she points her toes toward skyward and tucks her arms close to her body. She begins to increase her speed as her body streamlines, reducing drag, projecting herself swiftly downward.

Sam and Caesar, drunk with excitement for the thrill of the chase, happily accept the challenge. They begin to bark and howl into their comms as they begin their walk toward the end of the plane. Then, one after the other, they jump and flip into the air out the back of the plane.

After Sam and Cesar exit the rear of the plane, Eric begins to walk with Grace toward the plane's rear.

"Ready?" Eric asked Grace.

Although this was the first and worst cargo flight she had ever flown, she wasn't exactly sure she was ready to jump out of it either. Grace nods to Eric, takes a deep breath and then jumps off the lowered door unceremoniously. Eric counts to three to give her room and then leaps into a somersault into the emptiness of the sky. Toward the end of his slow-controlled tumble, Eric catches a glimpse of the plane as it slowly banks into a turn and heads back to the base.

CHAPTER XX

THE CAMP SITE

The team had all landed safely and had set up camp for the night. Eric caught a glimpse of something large moving around silently in the shadows. He wasn't sure, but whatever it was sent a chill up his neck. He knew something menacing was out there.

"I am going to take a leak and scout around a bit," Eric tells the team.

After Eric leaves, Darryl looks around to confirm that there is a little distance between Eric and their campsite. He then begins to smile mischievously.

"Fellow Hounds, to celebrate our reunion mission, I brought a little something to help christen the moment," Darryl expresses gleefully.

He reaches down into his backpack and pulls out four brown vials. He hands one to Sam and another to Caesar. Max reaches out her hand, but Darryl intentionally reaches past her and hands a vial to Grace. Max, realizing his intention, loses her smile and leans back. Darryl pops open his vial and starts drinking. Grace takes a sip, coughs uncontrollably, and hands the vial to Max as she utters,

"Whoa, is that paint thinner? I haven't had anything like that since college."

Max takes the vial, takes a drink, swishes it around in her mouth, and swallows it in one gulp. She hands the vial back to Grace, who waves it off. After a moment of drinking, Darryl is feeling emboldened from his vial of liquid courage. He decides to exact a little revenge on Max for her part in causing Eric to get arrested and kicked out of the Corps. He reaches over and taps Sam on the knee. Feeling a little buzzed, Sam looks over at Darryl.

"Watch this," Darryl says to Sam.

"Max, I dare you to kiss Grace," Darryl suddenly exclaims.

Sam and Caesar lower their vials and look in the direction of Max and Grace. Grace starts blinking slowly; she is made uncomfortable by the sudden attention. She knew Max would let them have it with a bit of her Puerto Rican flare. She turns to face Max and assesses her reaction. To Grace's surprise, Max moved closer to her and stared long into her eyes, similar to the way Max looked at her on the plane. Grace, unsure if Max was feeling giddy with the alcohol, decides to accept the vial this time as Max again motions for her to drink. Grace takes a sip from the vial. After a moment, she starts to feel a little light-headed.

"Just a small kiss. Grace doesn't mind," Darryl states.

As Max's eyes closed romantically, she tilted her head and started to lean in close to Grace's face. Under the influence of alcohol, Grace's mode went from uncomfortable to slightly open to exploration. Grace wasn't exactly sure how she was feeling about this, but she decided to go with it. She thought to herself, and I could always claim it was the alcohol later. Grace relaxed, closed her eyes, and began to lean in toward Max. Come to think of it, so far, this mission is starting to remind me more and more of those college years. Grace continued to think to herself.

Their lips were slowly getting close. Sam and Caesar's eyes widened, and their mouths began to open in shock. Darryl began to smile a devilish smile. He had won this round, he thought to himself.

Their lips were so close, just about to touch, when Max quickly turned her head away from Grace. Now facing Darryl, she gave him the one-finger salute with two hands as she angrily stood up and walked down the path Eric started on his patrol. All the guys started laughing and pointing at Darryl.

"What an idiot, you really thought Max was going to do it!" Said Sam.

"A brother has dreams," Darryl said.

"Yeah, wet ones!" Sam shot back laughing.

With that comment, everyone started roaring with laughter. Everyone except Grace, who was feeling sincerely humiliated by the team she thought of as family. She furiously got up, picked up her bag, and then walked away from the encampment. As that moment of everyone laughing at her played over and over in her mind, she found a big rock to sit on. Out of habit, she removed her laptop from her backpack, opened it, and placed it on her lap. Then, for a moment, she glanced up at the night sky. How at peace the stars must be, shimmering points of light in the darkness, she thought to herself. One of her favorite classes in college was astronomy, where she learned to pick out constellations. From her current position, she could make out Orion's belt.

Grace went back to her laptop after a brief glimpse at the sky. When she lowered her head to turn on her laptop, she realized there was a bright red luminous glow reflecting off the laptop screen. Grace thought it odd; maybe there was a swarm of glowing bugs approaching. But, before she could turn to see what was glowing so brightly behind her, the searing pain of what felt like jagged knives sinking into her neck reached her brain. Her laptop fell from her lap, and the screen cracked when it hit the ground as Grace was wrenched off the large rock by her neck and slammed onto the ground backward. She could taste dirt in her mouth as she was thrust backward. The force of her body hitting the ground sent dirt flying into the air and into her mouth.

Something had a hold of her; she couldn't tell what it was. All she could see was the bright red luminous glow around her. She could also feel its hot breath breathing in and out on the back of her neck. The creature paused, possibly to get a better hold; warm blood raced down her neck as the jaws of this creature collapsed her neck so severely she could barely breathe. She wanted to scream, but she was in too much pain, and she found it was becoming hard to get enough air. Grace felt this was her only chance to fend off whatever had a hold of her. She instinctively attempted to reach for something to hold onto to keep from being dragged off or to use as a weapon. Desperately pawing at the ground with her left hand, her backpack was the only thing she could reach. She grabbed onto it and held tight.

She tried to resist blacking out but could only use the rest of her strength to hold onto the object in her grasp. Grace could sense the pressure around her neck was slowly cutting off more of her oxygen; the world around her was starting to become smaller and dimmer. She got one last look at the night stars and Orion's belt before everything went black.

In the darkness, the hair of this creature that glowed bright red as it attacked Grace slowly began to dim as Grace began to lose consciousness. Suddenly the red glow dissipated, and the giant creature silently dragged Grace further into the darkness, away from the camp. Her backpack, body and blood left a small trail into the night.

CHAPTER XXI

THE CALM NIGHT

Max tracks down Eric and finds him relieving himself on a nearby tree. She doesn't bother to wait for Eric to zip himself up before she starts pointing her finger at him and speaking.

"You need to control your dogs, Eric, or I'll do it," she says in anger.

Eric begins to zip his pants and turns toward her.

"Calm down, Max. What's going on?"

Max pauses before she continues and looks Eric up and down.

"Aren't you going to rinse your hands?" Max asked, looking down at Eric's hands.

"What?" Eric asked, slightly confused.

Eric pulls out his canteen and pours water on his hands.

"¡Hombres no están limpios!" Max says, shaking her head, suddenly distracted.

"What's going on, Max?" Eric asks again, interrupting her.

A red flare penetrates the stillness of the night sky. Eric doesn't hesitate; he immediately drops the canteen he held, and pushes past Max as he runs as fast as he can back towards their campsite. Max spins around, pulls her handgun from her side and follows directly behind Eric.

Eric arrives at the camp panting; they hear Sam calling them.

"Over here."

Eric rushes in the direction of Sam's voice. When the duo reaches Sam, he motions for them to follow him cautiously. They arrive at the rock where Grace last sat before her abduction. Darryl is holding Grace's broken laptop. Everyone is looking distraught. As Eric approaches, Darryl is the first to speak.

"Eric, from the look of these broken branches, she didn't go willingly. There's blood behind the rock here. "

"Whoever took her better pray to their god for a quick death," Eric says angrily.

"Sorry, man, I should've been watching her," Darryl says apologetically.

There is a trail of blood showing where she was dragged off.

"I don't think it was a person. Look here." Sam says

Kneeling, Sam points next to the trail.

"There are huge paw prints. Nothing like I've seen back home, but definitely a large predator - may be a lion or something bigger."

"What's larger than a lion?" Cesar asks, with no anticipation of an answer.

As he stands, Sam notices something glowing on the broken brush branches. He removes it from the brush to examine it closer.

"It looks like hair or fur, but I've never seen any creature whose fur glows in the dark."

He hands it to the others to examine. Then, Eric tells the team about his almost deadly encounter with the one-eyed creature whose mane glowed like fire back at the abandoned church.

"I didn't mention this before because I thought you guys might think I was going crazy," Eric admitted.

"This is getting weird," Cesar mentions.

"It's almost as strange as those conspiracy stories Darryl is always going on about," Sam says in disbelief.

"I'm not sure what's going on, but it must have something to do with Global Unity's biohazard material. Sam, is there enough here to track her?" asked Eric.

"Sorry Eric, I already looked. The trail just ends," replies Sam.

"Where's her backpack? Is it missing?" Max asked while glancing around.

Wondering where her question was leading, Eric asks,

"Why is that important?"

"I slipped a tracker in her backpack when she fell into my lap on the plane," Max states

Suspiciously, Eric then asked,

"Wait! Why would you do that?"

Max spoke loudly enough for everyone to hear as she gave Darryl the side-eye.

"I knew your team didn't want me on this mission. I reasoned you'd never intentionally abandon Grace. So, I figured tracking her was my insurance to get back home if things went south."

After saying this, she softened her tone and walked up to Eric. She looked into his large brown eyes. She now knew that he had built up an affinity for Grace and needed to protect her for some reason. However, she didn't know why, but that answer would have to wait. She figured it was time to get her mission back on track.

"Are we going to argue about my methods, or are we going after Grace?" Max stated rhetorically.

CHAPTER XXII

THE CAVE ENTRANCE

Large rocks and shrubbery provide cover for the team. Eric uses binoculars to get a better view.

"Are you sure this is the right location?" Eric asked lightly to Max as he crouched down by her side.

"Well, at least her backpack is in there," Max answered, looking down at her tracking device.

Eric then turns to Darryl; Darryl looks questioning at the cave opening.

"Alright Hell Hounds, the mission is to locate Grace, recover the stolen material and get back to the rendezvous location." Eric barks to his team.

The team loads up their gear and then jumps into the Hummer. They drive cautiously as they approach the mouth of the cave. Not detecting any forms of resistance, Eric sizes up the cave entrance and drives into the cave.

As the hummer enters the cave, Eric notices something familiar. Carved into the rock above the cave is a symbol. Eric can't quite remember where he had seen this before.

$$\hbar$$

The team drove into the cave as far as the hummer would fit. They decided to disembark and walk the rest of the way. But first, the team unloaded their flashlights, gear, and guns.

The team reached a dead end in the cave.

"Is this right?" Cesar asked.

"The tracker shows we're right on top of her," Max answers rhetorically.

"There's nothing here," Darryl says.

"We must be missing something. Everyone spread out and search everything," Eric says as he moves the light of his flashlight around.

"Eric, over here. I think I found something." Shouts Sam.

Sam taps the cave wall in front of him with his flashlight.

"Do you hear that echo? There's something behind this wall." Sam tells Eric.

Sam and Eric shove the wall. Surprisingly, the wall moved easily. It moved back and then to the side as if on rollers, revealing a winding staircase.

"We don't know what we're walking into, so everyone keep a tight formation," Eric orders the team.

He then takes the lead down the stairs into the darkness. The team follows, tactically using their flashlights to light the way.

As they reached the bottom of the stairs and entered a passageway, Eric noticed that the walls of the cave became smoother.

They then came upon a wall with a symbol, a star map, and some inscriptions…

$$\hbar$$

nem et renascentiam templum mortis

"What is this symbol?" Sam asked.

"I can barely make out one of these writings. It says something like the temple of death or rebirth. Not really sure," Cesar says inquisitively.

"Ignore it. Stay focused on finding Grace." Eric tells the team.

Eric hears noises and sees the light at the end of the passageway. He signals the team to stop and take positions behind some rubble.

CHAPTER XXIII

THE HIDDEN TEMPLE

The team found themselves at the top level of an amphitheater-like space. It was a well-lit area, with four white columns supporting the ceiling. A large, stage-like platform was at the bottom level, with many bodies busily moving about. They appear to be in some sort of temple. The team took cover behind a pile of rubble from a fallen wall.

"Scan this area; see if you can locate Grace." Eric orders.

The team scans the area through their scopes to better assess their position. Eric spots a large pool-like area, slightly larger than forty feet long and twenty feet wide, filled with a thick, black oily substance. The pool was about a step below the stage and located diagonally across from the team, to the left. The surface of the liquid had a silvery sheen, and bubbles gurgled at the top. It was similar to a tarpit that animals would get trapped in.

Darryl, scanning in the direction directly to the right of the stage, discovers the first group of mercenaries sent by Dominik to retrieve their company's stolen product. The men were locked in cells carved into the rock walls. Furthest away from the team was the west wall of the temple, containing another cell holding what appeared to be the enormous one-eyed deformed lions. There was a zealot standing near the cage entrance. Darryl could see that the zealot's face was covered in white clay and similar face markings as the other zealots they came across during their initial mission in the desert.

On the temple wall behind the stage were two drawings, one of which was of a handsome male giant wearing a tunic, with children happily gathered around him. One of the children sat on the giant's knee. The other drawing scene was a dark drawing with the exact giant figure, except he appeared ragged. His beard and hair were now messy, and he had a wide-eyed stare akin to a monstrous giant. He grasped one of the children's limp bodies as he bit the head off.

The same symbol Eric was starting to become familiar with was carved into the wall underneath the drawing. In between the lion cell and the black pool was a passageway carved into the rocks. Still, there was no sign of Grace.

ℏ

Drums and chanting began to sound as if a performance had begun. Keeping their position hidden, Eric and the team realized that they had stumbled upon a strange ritual taking place.

"Darryl, you're the conspiracy nut. What's going on here?" Eric demanded.

Darryl looked at Eric, surprised by the question.

"Sorry, this sort of thing wasn't covered on my YouTube channel," Darryl said sarcastically.

One hooded figure in the middle of the commotion prompted Eric's attention. He seemed significantly taller than the other zealots walking around. He also seemed calm and more intent than the zealots roaming around. He stayed near the center of the platform next to a stand with an engraved box sitting on it. Eric thought to himself, if the other figures are of average height, the one orchestrating the events must be over seven feet tall. That figure also seemed to be broader than the others as well. Due to the hooded robe, Eric couldn't make out the figure's face as he walked around.

"The hooded figure in the center with the bright red robe is some sort of leader or high priest," Eric said, speaking in a low concealed voice.

"There's the missing mercs Dominik sent us to locate." Darryl pointed out.

"They're pretty bloody and badly beaten," Sam adds.

"No sign of Grace," says Cesar.

Two figures, who seemed to be lower priests, approached the cell where the three mercenaries were being detained. As one of the priests opens the cell, the mercenaries begin to scurry away in fear; however, their retreating was halted by the wall at the rear of the cell. Another zealot steps inside and grabs the most badly beaten prisoner. The team can hear him yelling, begging for mercy as he gets carried towards the high priest. Eric wondered what could've transpired to make hardened mercenaries act in such a terrified manner.

While the zealot approaches the high priest, he shoves the prisoner to his knees in front of the robed high priest. A large, pale albino hand appears from within the robe's sleeves; the hand seizes the kneeled mercenary by his jaw and squeezes forcefully. The lower priest began chanting. The team was able to hear it as if the shape of the temple seemed to amplify the deep chanting of the priest for all to hear. Tears pour down the face of the prisoner.

"Cesar, can you understand what he's saying?" Eric asks.

"Barely, it sounds similar to Latin and a few other tongues. It could be...'Thank you for your sacrifice' or, 'He's the sacrifice?'"

In the cell where the large, one-eyed mutant lions were being held, the zealot standing near the cage entrance was snapping a whip while shouting commands to the creatures, forcing them to back away from the opening of the cage. The beasts growl and roar in protest. Finally, after the mutant lions begin retreating towards the cell's rear, a zealot opens the cage. Eric noticed that one of the creatures had a wounded eye. He figured this was the lion he had battled back in the desert.

The high priest, who wore a brightly colored robe with many golden ornate symbols, stands to the side and watches as the two zealots pick up the battered mercenary and carry him to the cell holding the mutant lions. They shove him inside the creatures' cell like an unwanted rag doll. As the starving beasts smell the blood of the mercenary, their manes turn from an ordinary brown color to a glowing bright red. Then, in unison, the beasts pounce onto their helpless victim. As the beasts tear into the bruised flesh, a thick pool of blood slowly pours out of the cage. The mercenary yells out in agony as he's eaten alive. The hungry beasts then begin to swipe at each other as they fight for dominance and the right to devour the remains of the mercenary.

Eric clenches his teeth and balls up his fist angrily. His fingers push into his palm as he remembers only too well that he was once on the receiving end of those teeth. He was now convinced that these religious nuts sent the beast to attack them, and he wanted to make them pay.

"Poor bastard, he didn't deserve that," Darryl said somberly.

The high priest, unfazed by the gruesome events, walks over to an engraved box on a stand. Again, a pair of albino hands venture from the sleeves of the long, red intricate robe. He opens the box slowly, revealing a mystical dagger and several vials containing a thick black substance. The head priest begins to chant louder as the gleaming ceremonial dagger is lifted from the box. Then, balancing the handle in one hand and the knife's blade in the other, the pale hands ceremoniously hand the knife to a lower priest.

More zealots open the mercenary prisoners' cell and grab the two remaining, badly beaten men, one of whom appeared to be wearing military dog tags around his neck. They try to resist but are too weak to put up much of a fight. The zealots drag them from the cell and over to a set of chains and cuffs hanging from the top of the temple. The hanging chains were attached to a pulley operated by two zealots. The two men's wrists were handcuffed to the chains and pulleys with their hands above their heads. The lower priest signaled to the zealots, and they began to pull the chains. They stopped pulling once the two men began dangling a few feet in the air.

The lower priest walks over to the barely conscious mercenaries and pierces each of their sides. The men yell out in agony as their blood pours out of the wounds. Next, the priest captures their blood in ceremonial bowls. After enough blood has filled the bowls, he walks toward the high priest, kneels, and holds the bowls out as an offering. The high priest selects one of the bowls and holds the bowl close to the hood to savor its contents. He then tilts his head back slightly to drink. Eric, disgusted by the scene, was still unable to glimpse the face under the robe.

The high priest takes a vile from the box and the other bowl from the lower priest. He pours some of the liquid from the vile into the bowl. The high priest waves his hands over the bowl and chants. The lower priest walks back to the shackled mercenaries and, using a black chalky substance, places a symbol on the victims' foreheads and forces both of them to drink their own blood.

"Bingo, there's the corporation's property," Max states while looking through her scope.

Cesar pulls the cross he wears on a necklace from underneath his camouflage clothing, whispers a prayer to himself as he makes a symbol of a cross on his body.

Both men choke and gag but swallow the concoction in their weakened state. With that final act, other zealots maneuver the two gagging and choking men over the surface of the dark bubbling pool of *living* tar. The lower priest signals to the zealots manning the chains and pulleys, who then slowly move the men over the shimmering dark liquid. As the men are lowered into the pool, the shimmering black surface of the pool begins to convulse back and forth vigorously.

Seemingly unable to do anything, Eric and his team can only watch the events unfold through their scopes. When the men are a few feet from the surface of the black liquid, the shimmering black liquid reaches upward, grabbing hold of the prisoner's legs. Next, it begins creeping up their feet as it pulls them down into itself. The men began screaming when the black liquid grabs on to them.

White smoke appears as their clothes and skin dissolve when they come into contact with the black liquid. The zealots manning the pulleys begin straining to hold onto the chains under the force exerted on the mercenaries by the black liquid. Finally, the mercenaries were violently jerked under the surface by the bubbling shimmering liquid. When the screaming stopped, the silence was deafening.

Sam rubs his eyes in disbelief at what he just witnessed.

"Was that acid?" What's going on here?"

CHAPTER XXIV

THE RESCUE

Max, not being able to watch anyone else get tortured, nudges Eric.

"Eric, I am going to retrieve the remaining vials. Cover me," Max states bluntly.

"Are you crazy? If you are captured, it'll put us all in danger. Let's formulate a plan first," Eric orders.

"I did, and this is it," Max said defiantly.

Max jumped over the broken low-lying stone wall that the team used as a cover and started her march toward the platform below, where the vials were located. Darryl quickly turns toward Eric with bulging eyes. Eric knew that this was Darryl's *WTF* just happened look.

The high priest, with his face still hidden, turns around to face more of the zealots below his platform. He waves his pale hands and beckons them to move forward and gather around him. From the western passageway, Grace is escorted into the room. Clumps of blood mat her red hair. The high priest turns as she enters the room. The priest approaches Grace, and for the first time speaks loud enough for the gathering zealots to hear.

"Drink from the pool of transformation, become something greater and let the power of Saturn set you free." The high priest bellows from deep within the hood.

Grace looks into the hood of the high priest and begins to recoil away in fear. The high priest then gestures toward a set of chains and handcuffs being lowered down from the ceiling. Grace begins shaking her head in disbelief.

"No, this isn't real," she repeats to herself.

The robed lower priests approached her. They grab her by the arms and lead her toward the chains near the edge of the shimmering black pool. She looks around at the gathering crowd with skulls painted on their faces, and begins to weep with fear that she's about to die. The lower priests reach for Grace's wrist and begin to lift them above her head to shackle her into the cuffs. As if something had taken their attention away from her, Grace is surprised when the lower priests pause to look past her. Although weak, Grace unwittingly turns her head. A glimmer of hope comes over her. What she could make out was a bright, slightly wavering red dot on the high priest's chest. She knew what that meant. The gathering zealots immediately turn to search for the source of the beam.

Max menacingly walks toward the gathering crowd. Then, as if parting the red sea, the large group of zealots move to allow her to walk in between them. Her gun was firmly placed at her shoulder, and her laser pointed at the heart of the prominent hooded high priest. The lower priests put their hands on the knives at their sides to defend the high priest as Max moved forward to approach the steps leading up to the platform. The high priest's pale hand slowly signals to the lower priests to remove their hands from their weapons.

Behind the low-lying barrier, Eric sees Grace being escorted to the chains through his scope. He uses hand signals to the team to keep their eyes on him. He then leaps over the small rubble.

After stabilizing his rifle on the rubble and placing his finger on the trigger, Darryl shakes his head and says to himself,

"It's always bad luck to sleep with one of your teammates."

Max continues her advance towards the high priest. A voice sounds from the hood of the high priest's robe.

"Una mujer soltera? Debes estar enojada para venir aquí sola." The high priest bellows from within the hood.

"Tu hablas Español?" Max said, surprised to hear her language spoken.

"Sorry to disappoint you, but I'm not single. I already have a date with me," Max responds in English.

As she spoke to the high priest, another red dot appeared on his chest. The high priest lifts his gaze beyond Max. With his rifle securely placed at his shoulder, Eric approaches Max's position. The zealots bare their teeth, grimacing toward Eric as he carefully walks through them.

"Grace…Walk slowly over to me?" Eric says, keeping his focus squarely on the high priest.

Grace nods in agreement to Eric and looks around to verify it is safe. Then, cautiously, she walks away from the lower priests who were about to shackle her, then down the platform steps to where Eric stood.

"You dare interrupt the transformation ritual! You would take that which has been promised to end this pitiful world?" the high priest angrily shouts.

Attempting to be free of their captivity and join the fight, the beasts in the cell growl fiercely and start thrashing against the bars of their cages. Eric simultaneously notices some zealots slowly maneuver their hands onto the hilts of their knives.

"Not so fast," Eric warns the zealots.

Eric slowly releases his trigger finger and raises his hand to his shoulder; he then holds up two fingers. The lower priests next to Grace look at their robes and notice red dots appear on each other's chests.

"I didn't come alone either," Eric exclaims confidently.

Placing his finger back on the trigger of his rifle, releasing his other hand, Eric places it on Max's shoulder to let her know they were in the proper position.

"Diablo, if you so much as breathe too hard, I will turn you into a used Mexican piñata," Max stated in a threatening tone.

Taking a few steps forward, Max begins to walk up the platform steps. She reaches the box containing the vials and opens it. She reaches into the box, grabs the vials, places them one by one in a pocket under her Kevlar vest. After grabbing all the vials and securing them, she begins her retreat cautiously backward to Eric's position. She does this without taking her focus off the high priest. As she approaches, Eric places his hand on her shoulder to let her know she is back in position.

Eric then whispers in her ear, "This still isn't a date."

He slowly removes his hand from Max's shoulder, places his hand on Grace's back, and moves her into position between himself and Max.

Like trained beasts, the zealots kept still. They sneered at Eric and Max in a threatening manner as they passed between them. Eric could see the blood lust in their eyes. He knew they would sacrifice themselves if ordered. He hopes they can get back to their defensible position before that order is given.

Before the trio took another step to retreat away from the zealots, the high priest slowly started to move his pale albino hands toward his hood. He intentionally moved the hood slowly backward not to antagonize the intruders. Eric paused for a moment to catch a glimpse of the face hiding beneath that hood. As the hood finally fell, revealing the high priest's face, Eric wished he hadn't paused to look.

The high priest's head was covered in colorless pale white skin that matched his hands. His head was large and elongated, with one sole, large eye in the center of his forehead. He had no eyelashes, eyelids, or eyebrows. The single eye contained a red pupil that singular transfixed on Eric. The high priest stuck out an abnormally long tongue to lick his lips. He then folded his arms across his chest in defiance. After seeing his face, Eric felt his heart skip a beat. The high priest didn't have any lips, and his teeth were exposed when he began speaking. They were sharp, jagged, and resembled the teeth of a wild animal.

"As the High Priest, I represent the ancient, dark Gods of Saturn. They came here centuries ago, and their consciousness remains in an embryonic state inside the pool of transformation. As humans enter the pool, those that are worthy receive gifts of higher consciousness. Those who are found unworthy become mindless corpses."

The High Priest raises his left arm and motions towards Grace.

"We have awaited her arrival as part of the Gods' plan to cover the Earth in darkness. So, give back the tribute, and perhaps we will let you live." The high priest threatened the trio.

What was he? Eric thought to himself. He now understood why Grace and the mercenaries were so scared. But, Eric did not understand what the high priest was speaking of and certainly wasn't waiting around to figure it out.

Max was horrified by the sight of him. She was caught off guard as she failed to calculate a giant one-eyed man into her plan. Even still, she kept her composure.

The rest of the team behind the rubble remained focused as their training kicked in, and they awaited Eric's signal.

"Damn, Cesar, I thought *you* were ugly," Darryl says while looking through his scope.

"That's not what your sister said last night." Cesar shot back calmly without taking his focus off his scope.

Eric periodically glanced down at the hands on the knives on the hips of the zealots. He knew from experience that they were highly skilled at using them. Then, he notices a zealot to his right begins unsheathing his knife; Eric quickly steps in front of him and butts him in the nose with the end of his gun. The zealot quickly falls to his knees in pain, his eyes shut from the sudden pain. He tastes the blood from his nose that now rushed over his lips into his mouth.

After Eric makes his move, Max seizes the right hand of a zealot, twists his wrist, turns him around, and holds him directly in front of her. As he struggles to free himself, she kicks him in the back of the knee, forcing him to kneel on the ground.

Grace knew to keep her position directly in between Eric and Max. She had been in this situation before and knew it would quickly escalate into a life-or-death situation.

To Max's left, she catches a glimpse of a figure starting his advance. One step was all he took as she spotted him, firmly squeezing her trigger and hitting the approaching zealot in the chest. The close range and force of her shot propels him backward, and he slips into the black pool. His flesh dissolves off his bones, and white smoke appears as the liquid consumes him.

Eric, facing the direction of the one-eyed priest once again, notices another zealot attempting to rush toward them. It was only briefly that he noticed the red dot before his attacker hit the floor.

More zealots were running towards them from all directions. Max and Eric opened fire as they sped up their retreat.

Under the distraction of gunfire, the giant, one-eyed albino high priest slyly walks down the platform toward the edge of the black oily pool. As he does this, he lifts his massive albino arms, his palms opened to the ceiling, and begins chanting out loud as his one eye rolls to the top of his head.

Grace frantically pounds her head,

"Stop it! Stop calling my name!" she repeats in a low but distressed voice.

"Get out of my head!"

"Grace, pull it together. This is not the time to freak out!" Eric yells at her while firing rounds into charging zealots.

CHAPTER XXV

THE RETREAT

Darryl scans the area with his scope to ensure no zealots have located their position. He spots something strange at the edge of the black oily pool. As he adjusts his scope to get a closer view, he is surprised at what appears to be mangled black fingers gripping the rim of the pool. Rubbing his eyes and blinking before peering back into his scope, he now sees what appears to be a human-like head slowly rising out of the black liquid. Suddenly, he sees another pair of hands on the rim, then another head centered between that pair of hands. Subsequently, two more heads rise next to those, then four more near those. Darryl could see dog tags hanging off the necks on two of the partially dissolved bodies. Their empty eye sockets glowed intensely red like fire. Darryl rubs his eyes again in disbelief.

Darryl jerks Cesar from his kneeling position and points in the direction of the pool.

"What in God's name is that?" Darryl mutters.

Cesar turns his scope in the direction Darryl pointed out. He is unable to understand what he's seeing. Cesar jabs Sam, who becomes instantly annoyed at having his concentration broken. Cesar gestures with two fingers in the direction of the pool. Sam quickly turns his scope to the side of the pool. While Sam views the activity at the pool, Cesar pulls his holy cross on a necklace from under his Kevlar jacket again and kisses it. There were now many more heads rising out of the oily black pool.

Many of these grotesque figures were now entirely out of the pool and advancing in the team's direction behind the rubble. They were covered in the black goo from which they emerged. They wore tattered pieces of clothing; some wore necklaces, others had one sandal, and pieces of their flesh were missing, exposing black stained bones. Darryl was witnessing something he couldn't explain. The only word Darryl could find in his mind to describe these events was…

"Evil," Cesar said out loud, firmly grasping his cross.

Max arrived back at the location the team had used for cover. She quickly jumped over the low laying rubble wall, picked up her rifle, and aimed it back in the area of her retreat. Eric helped Grace over as she started mumbling to herself. Their backs were toward the pool and were completely unaware of the strange activity at its edge. Darryl stood up and stared off into the distance beyond Eric. Darryl could now plainly see the mangled mobs of flesh approaching. Knowing Darryl didn't become alarmed quickly, Eric turned and looked through his scope to see what consumed his attention.

"God bless America!" Eric exclaimed.

Eric, shocked at the sight of the advancing grotesque bodies, fires around in the direction of the approaching horde. The bullet hits one of them in the shoulder; unfazed, it keeps advancing. After that shot, the entire team takes a defensive position behind the wall then unleashes a flurry of rounds on the advancing disfigured, lifeless beings steadily approaching them. Every one of their rounds finds its target, but still, they keep advancing.

"Are those people?" Sam questions out loud.

Grace answers weakly as the voices in her head fade.

"Those people are all dead. They are living corpses. Once they enter the black pool, which is a bio substance, they become one collective mind. To make matters worse, the high priest controls them."

In disbelief, the team continues firing until the lifeless mob becomes too close for the team's safety. The remaining zealots, realizing the intruders were at a disadvantage, pull their knives from their belts and begin running and screaming towards the team's position. The one-eyed giant priest signals to open the cages containing the excited beasts. The beasts roar with delight as they are set free once again. The mutant lion with the wounded eye attacks the zealot with the whip; two others knock down a few zealots as they run towards Eric and the team's position.

Eric, noticing the zealots, beast, and living corpses approaching their position, lifts Grace to carry her and exclaims,

"Time to move!"

Without hesitation, the team gathers their guns and packs and then scrambles out of their hiding place. In their haste to escape the onslaught and hordes of enemies, no one bothered to turn on their flashlight.

Living corpses aggressively clawed at each other's flesh as they attempted to enter into the narrow passageway. In a state of bloodlust, a zealot pushed his way into the middle of the living corpses. One of the living corpses grabbed hold of his right shoulder and his arm. Another living corpse grabbed his torso. The zealot attempted to get free, but he couldn't move. A living corpse in front of the zealot turned around to face him and quickly bit into his face. The zealot screamed as blood ran down his cheek. As he fell to his knees, other living corpses bit into him. The hoard momentarily paused their progression forward as they continued to bite into the flesh that dared get in their way.

Eric and his team attempt to retrace their path back down the dimly lit passage and could hear the unholy screams from the zealot being eaten alive and the roars of the beasts.

Darryl, who was protecting the team's rear, turned to see how much distance was between them and the oncoming terror, and he didn't like what he saw.

"Lock and load. They are coming fast!" Darryl shouted.

Darryl, Max and Sam turn to face the priest and living corpses while retreating backward as safely as possible. Facing the living corpses, they start relentlessly firing down the tunnel in the direction of the roars and horrifying screams from the advancing zealots. In the low light of the passageway, Darryl, Max, and Sam were unable to completely see what they were hitting. The only thing that was clearly visible was the haunting red glow of the living corpses' eye sockets as they continued to approach.

The trio continues firing their guns down the passageway into the sea of endless red eyes, who were now directly in front of them. Every spark of bullets released into the passageway momentarily lights up the area. In those few moments, Darryl, Sam, and Max could make out the disfigured faces. They had bloated rotting flesh with black ooze dripping from various parts of their bodies.

Darryl spies a set of red eyes climbing the walls to his right and left. Then the eyes move toward the ceiling. Darryl hits the one to his right but misses the other as it swiftly crawls over the top of the team.

"I don't believe this. These things are goddam roaches!" Darryl shouts in disbelief.

The living corpse that managed to escape Darryl's bullets drops down from the ceiling and lands directly in front of Eric and Grace. Although surprised, Eric is still able to hold Grace upright. The living corpse reaches out to grab Grace, but Eric is able to kick it with great force, causing it to fall to the ground. Cesar, noticing the action, fires a round into the living corpse's skull. The glowing red eye sockets dim and go out.

Eric, still holding Grace, stands with Cesar behind the other team members, guarding their rear advance. Focusing all their training to defend their lives, the team works as one as they rapidly fire down the tunnel.

As they retreat, the team passes a jutting wall and leans against it, using it as cover. They place their backs against the wall and peer out.

Max yells out after checking her rounds. "Out!"

Cesar hands her his gun and bends down to reload her gun. Sam steps forward to defend Cesar's position as Max begins another bevy of rounds against the living corpses. Seeing the living corpses up close was overly horrific for Cesar. His mind couldn't comprehend what was happening. In his state of fear, he yelled out,

"It's no use! These bullets aren't doing anything! They just keep coming!"

"Cesar, what are you doing? Stay focused. We're not dead yet!" Eric shouts from the other side of the passage.

The horde continues to advance.

"Sam, place some explosives here. Block their advance," Eric orders.

Sam opens up his backpack, pulls out two explosive devices, and places one on each side of the passageway.

"20 seconds!" Sam shouts.

The team stops shooting and runs as fast as they can down the passageway and up the stairs to the point of their initial entry. Max and Cesar start to roll the large stone door close. Darryl joins them and gets the stone moving faster. The team can feel the ground tremble as the explosive devices detonate against the stone walls as they close the door.

Eric bends slightly as he sets Grace down against the wall. Sam and Cesar bend over, panting as they attempt to catch their breath. Darryl walks over to Eric.

"It isn't safe to stay here. They're going to find a way around and into this cave. So let's get in the Humvee and haul ass out of here," Darryl says excitedly.

"He's right; we aren't safe here. We need a plan to destroy those things for good." Max adds as she interjects into the conversation.

Irritated, Darryl turns toward Max and states,

"Hopefully, a better plan than the one you had back at the temple."

Max angrily points her finger up toward Darryl's face.

"Screw you, I saw a chance, and I took it!"

She was a lot smaller than Darryl, but she was fierce, and she wasn't backing down.

Eric moved between Darryl and Max to diffuse the situation.

"That's enough!" Eric states emphatically.

"Sam, how many explosives do you have left?" Max asked.

Before Sam could answer, Eric barks,

"Max, our mission is over, and you're going to fly us out of here."

"I don't work for you, Eric. *Your* mission may be over, but I'm going back there to blow the temple and that black goo that turns people into mindless freaks. You *boys* can wait for me on the plane." She shoves her backpack into Eric's chest.

"Max, for once think! We aren't equipped to fight against the

crazed zealots, mutant-lions, and living corpses head-on." Eric
said forcefully, trying to rationalize with Max.

"Do you think we should let those...*things* get out of here and
wreak havoc on the world? You saw what they did to those mercs.
You remember the images we saw. Those things used to be people.
Imagine what that black goo will do to that nearby town. They
will all become mindless corpses."

Eric looks at Darryl for argumentative support. Darryl just
shrugs as he says,

"Hey, she can handle herself."

"I'm going with Max. I want to return the favor to those bastards
and keep Global Unity from getting their hands on that bio pool
substance," Grace says as she stands up slowly.

"I've never seen two people so anxious to die," Eric states, exhaustedly.

"Alright, let's go," Eric said, shaking his head.

He cared for Max and Grace, and he knew neither of them
would make it out alive, so he couldn't let them go alone. Nor
could he ask any of the other guys to go either.

Sam digs around his pack for his remaining explosives. Pulling
them out of his pack, he paused to look at Eric to ensure this was
what he wanted to do.

"I'll pre-set the timer for you." Sam begins. "Once you start the
timer, you'll have 20 minutes to get out of the temple, or you'll
miss the rendezvous permanently." He sets the digital timers and
hands the timers with the explosives to Max. She carefully places
them in her pack.

CHAPTER XXVI

THE LAST STAND

Eric reviews the plan for their return to the hidden temple. Realizing that they all should have weapons, he hands Grace a pistol.

"Do you remember how to use this?" Eric asks.

"Yes," Grace says with some hesitation.

Darryl moves into position to open the sliding cave wall. Sam stands directly in front of it, ready to shoot anything that dared to enter into the cave.

Eric speaks to Max,

"I'll go first and make sure the stairs and passageway are clear. Wait for the all clear."

Eric, Max, and Grace line up with their backs to the wall, adjacent to the opening. They wait as Darryl slides the wall back.

Eric immediately turns on his flashlight, then quickly passes through the opening. The remaining team members momentarily held their breath as Eric's footsteps trailed off.

"Clear," Eric called back to the cave.

Max and Grace slid through the opening. As soon as they entered, Darryl slid the wall back in place.

The trio cautiously walked down the stairs toward the passageway. The area was clear, with no signs of zealots or the living corpses. Strangely, they were able to enter the great hall without any resistance.

Max directs Grace and Eric to place the explosives on the temple ceiling pillars.

"We need to start the timers at the same time to sync the explosions," Eric adds.

Max hoped Sam had given them enough explosives to do the job.

Hoping she configured everything correctly, Grace called out nervously,

"Explosive in place."

"Ready here," Max calls out.

"Alright, one, two..." Eric calls out.

Before Grace could start her timer, the high priest sneaks in with two zealots from the side passage. One of the two zealots immediately grabs Grace, places a dagger to her throat and his hand over her mouth, and drags her back toward the high priest. The other zealot pulls out a knife and stands between the two opposing duos protecting the other's retreat. Max turns around and pulls out her sidearm. Pointing it at the zealot in front of her, Max speaks calmly but loud enough to get Eric's attention.

"We have a situation."

Knife in hand, the second zealot shuffles back and forth, challenging Eric and Max's advance toward the zealot holding Grace. Knowing he had the upper hand, the high priest folds his arms and demands, "Drop your primitive guns and kick them away." Max bends down to place her sidearm on the ground. She simultaneously and discreetly reaches behind her and starts the timer on her explosive device.

"If you go now, I'll let you leave safely," the high priest calls out to Eric and Max.

Eric places his sidearm on the floor, but he begins to remove his Kevlar vest when he stands up. He then holds up his fist and squares his position against the high priest.

"We're not leaving without Grace."

After watching Eric's skills earlier, The high priest could not resist the challenge. The priest unfastens his vibrant red robe, letting it fall to the floor, revealing his toned albino chest. He motions for the zealot still holding Grace to stand back as he rotates his shoulders and flexes his muscles in a show of intimidation.

The high priest signals to his zealots, and they start to slowly retreat backward toward the opening where they had entered.

"Eric, what are you doing? We don't have time for this machismo B.S." Max looks over her timer...18 minutes and counting down.

"Either we all leave, or none of us gets out," Eric called back while keeping his eyes intently focused on his opponent."

As Eric and the High Priest approach each other, Eric throws a quick punch that lands squarely on the side of the face of his adversary. The solid blow made a loud thud sound as their flesh met and the high priest's head thrust to the opposite direction. The punch landed with enough force to cause blood to flow from the high priest's lower lip. The high priest paused and released his serpent-like tongue to taste the blood.

"Come now... I am the high priest. Is that the best you could do?" said the high priest as he chuckled.

Eric's plan wasn't to win this fight; there was little chance of that. Max notices that Eric has the high priest's full attention and has drawn him away from Grace. She sprints towards the first zealot. Preparing for her charge, the zealot crouches and prepares to slash at Max's advance. When Max approaches, she steps on his bent knee to propel her up to his torso and then places her legs firmly around the zealot's neck. His head firmly between her thighs, she twists her body and leans her weight forward, propelling herself and her opponent to the floor. The zealot blacks out as the force of his skull meeting the floor sent a shock wave of pain to his brain. Max uses that same momentum to roll herself a few feet away from her unconscious opponent. Ending her roll, she turns her torso to face the zealot still holding Grace. Max stands and begins a sprint toward her next opponent.

The second zealot notices Max's charge towards him and Grace. The speed at which Max disposed of his ally made him realize he was in trouble. He turned in the direction of the high priest, and it was at that moment he saw his giant leader was too far away to offer help. Panicked, he hoped he could ward off Max's incoming attack by applying pressure to Grace's neck with his dagger. Tiny drops of blood began to appear. Max stopped right in front of the pair, raised her arms to her chest, jumped upward, and began a midair spin. From Grace's perspective, the entire scene unfolded quickly and in slow motion. She could see Max running and then leaping into the air. She thought her body was so perfectly symmetrical she looked like a ballerina performing a midair pirouette.

When Max finished her midair windmill kick, she planted her boot firmly across the zealot's chest, instantly propelling him back towards the floor and knocking the wind out of him. Unfortunately for the zealot, the force also dislodged the dagger from his hand. Max rushed to retrieve the dagger. The zealot writhed on the floor, attempting to find his breath. Max walked over to him, sat on top of his chest, and covered his mouth with her hand as she forced his dagger between his neck and shoulder blade. Grace squirmed and turned away. She had seen a lot of death recently, but she didn't think she would ever get used to watching someone die up close.

The high priest was happily exchanging blows with Eric when he heard the commotion between Max and the zealot. As he stepped back to square up his opponent, he turned his head slightly to track his zealots and noticed one unconscious on the floor. Stepping further back and turning in the other direction, he noticed Max standing next to Grace where his other zealot once stood. When he turned to face Eric again, Eric was triumphantly smiling. Now he understood Eric's plan, and he initially thought his adversary's constant retreat was in fear. However, the realization that Eric had tricked him enraged him. He clenched his fist, tensed his muscles, and his anger erupted into a beastly animalistic roar. The high priest charged, but Eric ducked under the charge and headed toward Max and Grace.

When Eric dodged the priest's rage-filled charge, he noticed that Max and Grace were now standing near the chains and levers used by the zealots on the mercenaries. His eyes met Max's, and he knew what she was trying to tell him. He turned to face his opponent once again, squared up his fighting stance, and began landing punch after punch to the giant's torso. He'd land a punch combo then retreat. He repeated this until he knew he was in the proper position.

The high priest was now so full of anger he was no longer feeling any pain. He raised an open hand and slapped Eric across the face to answer to Eric's punches. The giant's hand was so large the slap covered the entire side of Eric's face and temporarily stunned him. He saw stars as he staggered backward, but he focused on staying in position.

"You do not deserve to be fought as a human...I will defeat you like the dog you truly are," growled the high priest.

The high priest rushed Eric once again. In Eric's stunned state, he could not dodge the rapid charge. The high priest was able to grapple his hands through Eric's defense. The priest's large hands found their target and were now securely pressed around Eric's throat. The high priest smiled victoriously as he triumphantly lifted Eric off the ground by his neck. Eric's feet were now dangling in the air, and he was now gazing directly into the high priest's single eye with great disgust.

Eric felt the cold, lifeless hands slowly restrict his air as he attempted to break the high priest's grip from around his neck. He lifted his hands high above his head and slammed them into the giant's wrists. Again, Eric reached his hands high above his head and slammed them against the wrists of the high priest. He repeated this again and finally felt what his hands had been reaching for. He held on to them tightly, and rapidly brought his hands down; but this time he clamped steel shackles around the giant's wrists.

Max and Grace, who waited next to the chain pulley and crank, hoped Eric had understood their plan. As Eric clapped the shackles on the high priest, they both started turning the crank. This was the moment they were waiting for. They both quickly began to reel in the chain. The chain rattled as it tightened against the weight of the giant.

Instantly, the high priest's hands were jerked from around Eric's throat as the tightening chain forced his hands straight into the air. The priest was so massive that Max and Grace strained to exert enough force to hold the priest's arms in the air. Eric, trying to regain the air in his body, was dazed but haphazardly made his way over to Max. He grabbed the section of the chain leading to the crank and pulled with all the strength he could muster. He leaned his entire bodyweight backward and pulled downward. His muscles strained under the weight of the priest. The high priest's feet were dangling off the ground. It was Eric's turn to lift his opponent in the air.

"Go!" Eric shouted as sweat began to bead on his forehead.

They would only have one chance at this. Max and Grace began running towards the struggling high priest; as they ran, they gained momentum. Realizing what was happening, the high priest's single eye enlarged with panic as the female duo blitzed towards him. He frantically tried to get free of the shackles. Max and Grace, with all the momentum their petite bodies could muster, planted their shoulders into the body of the High Priest, propelling him outward over the pool of shimmering black goo. At that moment, Eric released his straining grip on the chain and fell backward to the floor from exhaustion. The crank spun wildly and rattled uncontrollably under the tremendous weight on the other end.

Once the priest's feet were close enough to descend into the pool, the black goo reached up and grabbed one of the legs of the widely flailing high priest. Grace stood near the pool's edge to watch the priest's body. He howled and hissed and yelled as his clothes and flesh began to dissolve into the black goo, and then silence. Grace wanted to vomit. She couldn't tell if it was the sight of the high priest's flesh dissolving off his bones, or the realization of the fate the high priest had for her.

"Arder en el Infierno!" Max yelled triumphantly before rushing over to Eric to help him to his feet.

Eric was in a bad state, as half of his face was blue, and his left eye was black and closed. He could barely open his right eye but smiled when Max approached his side. He could slightly make out Grace, who was several yards beyond Max.

"Time to move," Max barks loudly enough for Grace to hear.

Grace turns away from the pool and takes a few steps towards

Max and Eric. Just then, one of the explosive timers that Max had set reached double zero. A massive explosion destroys one of the pillars in the temple. After that, parts of the ceiling started falling, and cracks began to appear on the temple floor. At that moment, a sinkhole forms underneath Grace, and she falls through the floor and drops out of sight.

After larger pieces of the ceiling stop falling, Max helps Eric over to the spot where Grace dropped through the floor. They peer through the hole from where she fell when they reach the location. A single beam of light from the temple shined through the darkness. Eric and Max could see Grace was in what appeared to be another tunnel or cavern about ten to fifteen feet below them. She was cut, bruised from the jagged pieces of rock, and her right ankle appeared black and swollen.

"Grace, reach for my hand!" Eric shouts frantically.

He reaches down into the hole to offer Grace his hand. Grace, slightly dazed, responds to the sound of Eric's voice. When she opens her eyes, she sees the beam of light shining behind Eric. She thought she saw an angel reaching out to her for a slight moment. The angel was a bit far, but yet seemed so near. She extended her hand to reach out to her angel. Her hand trembled as she tried to hold it steady for the angel to grasp. "If I could only touch the angel, all this pain would finally be over." She thought to herself.

From within the passageway that Grace was trapped in, Max and Eric began to hear deep sounds getting louder in the distance. Eric immediately knew the sound meant that Grace was in danger.

"For God's sake, Grace, please reach for my hand!" Eric became frantic as the beastly growls became nearer.

Before Grace could reach her angel, she jerks her hand back

and places them on her head in agony.

"Stop calling my name! Get out of my mind!" Grace yells out as the pain in her head ripped her away from the vision of her angel.

From her left, she could hear the low growling as well. Frightened, Grace turned to her left. In the dim light, she could see the shadowy silhouette of what appeared to be a large lion with a huge mane. It walked lightly as it stalked her. Then, as it came closer, Grace noticed that it was wounded. Its eye was damaged. The beast's large mane and tail fur started to glow intensely red like a burning flame. It opened its massive jaws wide, and saliva dripped from its fangs. It sniffed the air as he sensed Eric's presence and growled threateningly before turning its attention back towards Grace.

Eric watches in horror as the beast slowly stalks Grace. The passageway lights up into a bright red glow as its hair glows fiercely red. Eric could see Grace's face now. The red light from the lion's main reflected off the left side of her face. Although bruised, Eric could see the softness in her skin and the tears running down her face. Grace felt helpless as she looked up at Eric and Max. Eric remembered his first meeting with her back at the base. She was so youthful and independent. He remembered how he taught her to hold a gun on the range.

Grace screams an eerie high-pitched scream as the one-eyed beast pounces onto her. Its colossal body completely covers hers, blocking Eric's and Max's view. The lion's glowing red mane stops glowing. Eric looks away from the scene. His eyes began to swell and moisten as tears began rolling down his cheek. He knows all too well what those beasts could do to a person. The grounds underneath Eric's tears were wet with despair.

"She's gone. That damn beast killed her!" Eric cries out.

With the bit of energy he had left, he balled up his fists and pounds them into the tear-stained rubble.

"We need to go. There's nothing we can do," Max says somberly as she helps Eric up.

THE SACRIFICE

Grace found herself being dragged, once again, by the lion-like beast. He left her in a dimly lit chamber, where she heard subtle sounds of liquid dripping from all around. The chamber floor and walls were made of rock but smooth. She looked around quickly and became frightened as she realized where she was. She had been dragged back to the chamber in the temple with the pool of black ooze.

She then noticed a pain in her arms.

"Is this my blood?" "Oh my god, I'm bleeding?"

She started yelling for help, hoping anyone could hear her.

"HELP! Someone!"

"Max, Eric, I'm hurt! I need help!"

She felt so helpless and alone. She started to cry.

Near the top of the chamber, directly across from her, she thought she saw something move. Grace became even more afraid.

She then started hearing the voices in her head, but they sounded slightly different. They appeared much clearer.

"We've been waiting for you. After your transition, you will help bring to fruition the final phase of our plan."

On one side of her, she could hear what sounded something close to growling. The same sound she heard right before some immense pain forced her unconscious. The beast, with the wounded eye, slowly stepped into the light near her. Growling threateningly, but not attacking. It was so close to her the entire time, yet she couldn't tell it was there at all.

Should I run for it? Grace pondered.

She thought running was her best option but to where? She was trembling and could barely see anything. She thought, I could run from this beast, but would that lead me to more beasts?

Suddenly, the beast lurched at her, she tried to cover her face for protection, but he grabbed one of her forearms with his teeth. She started screaming as pain leaped from her arms to her brain. As the beast started dragging her, she started screaming as loud as she could, flailing as hard as she could and kicking the ground to free herself in protest. She was like a rag doll in his grip. The beast kept hold of her forearm as she kept flailing. She wondered where it was taking her. Was she to be eaten by the beast? Finally, the beast stopped, and she realized what was happening. She was on the edge of that pool of black liquid.

In her panic state, the only thing she could think of was, why is this happening to me? She then hears the voice in her head.

"This will be the last time you ever cry. You will never feel weak or alone ever again."

The beast then drags Grace and itself into the dark liquid. Just for a moment, she could feel the liquid, almost like acid, burning the skin off of her arm. She wanted to scream, but she no longer had the will. Then, as the pool liquid reached her eyes, everything went black.

"So, this is death."